Praise for

Paul Beckman's *Peek*

Most of these flash stories are only a page or less in length, the shorter ones being the most impactful. In some cases, within the confines of a brief paragraph the author completes an emotionally charged arc where each of the characters are fully developed and stay with the reader after the story's completion. It is, in fact, Beckman's ability to sketch a character so completely with so few words, that makes these stories work as well as they do.

~ Matthew Hall, author of *The Human Condition Is A Terminal Illness* and *Pigeons and Peace Doves*

Beckman also plays with sound and smell. One of my favorites is 'Brother Speak'. Here are two brothers whose interactions raise stakes and tension with each subsequent paragraph. Pure Beckman. This is just a taste of what this author does with story and character. Because he wants to surprise the reader, play with you, shock you, make you laugh, make you *think*, I don't want to write too much more. Read for yourself.

~ Gay Degani, author of *What Came Before* and *Rattle of Want*

Moving seamlessly between voyeurs and Vespas, Kosher soap and secret lives, *Peek* goes from clever to heartbreaking to outright bizarre with equal dexterity. It's as if Woody Allen and Charles Bukowski got your favorite uncle hammered all weekend and made him spill the family dirt in perfect, flash fiction-sized bites.

~ Nancy Stohlman, author of *The Vixen Scream and other Bible Stories* and *The Monster Opera*

Beckman gives us no illusions about his characters. They are as flawed and basic as any of us, the caveat being that the reverse is also true. That's where the compassion and humor comes in, and comes in spades.

~ David S. Atkinson, author of *Apocalypse All the Time* and *Not Quite So Stories*

Beckman has created a creative and gripping collection of flash fiction ... The stories are all separate from each other, with a new voice for every new protagonist and a fresh storyline for every page. Beckman has given us a teasing peek into his writing and I'm hoping it won't be the only one.

~ Eleanor Hemsley in *Sabotage Reviews*

Some of these dark, ambitious stories of desire and anxiety are hilarious. In others the joke is on the startled reader, who has not quite anticipated how far our fellow creatures—and Beckman—will go.

~ Alice Mattison, author of *When We Argued All Night* and *Nothing Is Quite Forgotten in Brooklyn*

When picking up *Peek*, get ready for a look inside the subconscious of a unique cast of characters. Not only will they become endeared to you in such a short amount of words, but they'll make you start to wonder if you're really not all that different from them. Beckman gives you a peek, not only into the lives of fictional characters, but into the quirks of the universally damaged side of human nature.

~ Taylor Eaton, author of *God Gave Me Butterfly Wings* and *The Suicide of the Moon*

I wish I had written so many of these wonderful pieces. But the next best thing to writing a great story, is reading one, or two, or three ...

~ Michael C. Keith, author of *The Next Better Place* and *Life is Falling Sideways*

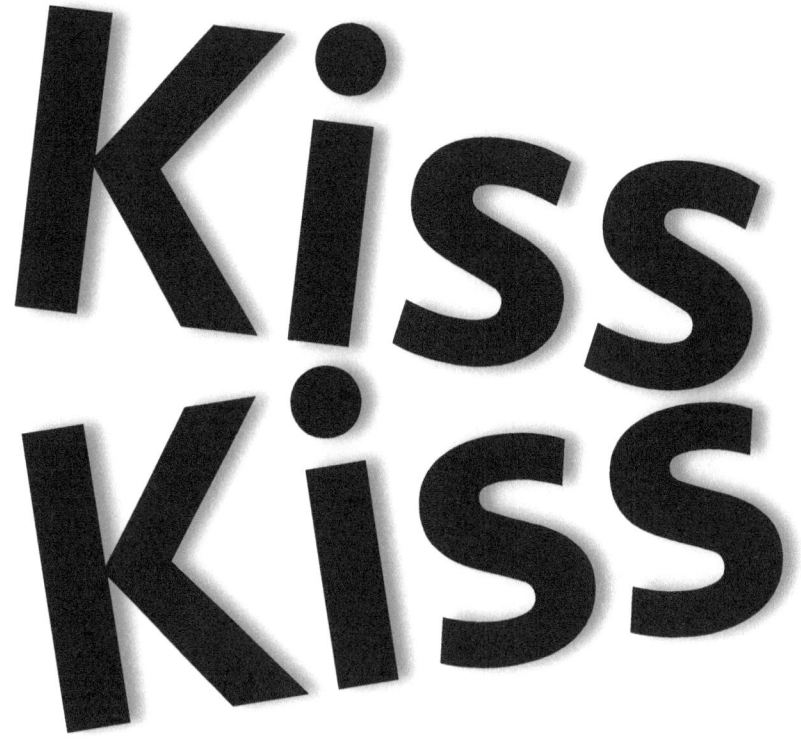

PAUL BECKMAN

TRUTH SERUM PRESS

ISBN: 978-1-925536-21-8

Truth Serum Press
32 Meredith Street
Sefton Park SA 5083
Australia

Email: truthserumpress@live.com.au
Website: http://truthserumpress.net
Truth Serum Press catalogue: http://truthserumpress.net/catalogue/

Original cover photograph copyright © Sebastian Villarroel
Author photograph copyright © Joshua Beckman
Cover design by and copyright © Matt Potter

Also available as an eBook
ISBN: 978-1-925536-22-5

Truth Serum Press is a member of the
Bequem Publishing collective
http://www.bequempublishing.com/

Also by Paul Beckman

Peek

Come! Meet My Family
and other stories

Lovers and Other Mean People

Maybe I Ought to Sit
in a Dark Room for a While

21 Stories

With gratitude to

Gay Degani
Kathy Fish
Nancy Stohlman

And those who were seen dancing
were thought to be insane by those
who could not hear the music.

Friedrich Nietzsche

Contents

With a Wink and a Nod

It was four days before my fifty-eighth birthday when my body started to fall apart. I was taking a late morning walk in the park when I felt strangeness after stepping down on my right foot. I hobbled to a park bench, took off my sneaker and shook it, thinking there was a pebble but there wasn't, so off came the sock and I checked out my foot. A toe was missing—my pinky toe. I stuck my hand in the sock and found it. A pinky toe's nothing to throw away so I put it in my pants pocket until I got home and then put it in the small canister from our unused canister set.

A few mornings later after my shower I was looking in the bathroom mirror and saw a black hair sticking out from my earlobe. I tugged it several times and my right earlobe popped off and was dangling from the hair. I put it in the canister with the pinky toe.

Last week I was on the turnpike, trying to move over to the right lane for my exit and a guy in a guard's uniform driving a large SUV wouldn't let me cross in front of him so I slowed down to go behind. He slowed down too, looked over at me and smirked. I flipped him the bird and my middle finger on my right hand went flying and bounced off the windshield onto the passenger seat floor. The guy gave me the finger back then sped off leaving me to barely make my exit. Once home, I washed my finger, dried it with a kitchen towel, and into the canister it went.

Next my left heel came off while I was in a shoe store trying on a pair of wingtips and that was followed by the bridge of my nose which came off in my index finger and thumb when I squeezed it while trying to remember something. Following that was my left eyelid from winking and the eyebrow above when I made a surprise face due to my eyelid. Then my mustache and upper lip came off while trimming my mustache. My chin dropped off as I bit into a Tootsie Pop and that filled up the canister.

I still went to work but had to have new ID badges made. My wife, Madge, decided I wasn't the same man she married some thirty-five years ago so she left and moved into our summer home on the lake. I got thinking about her one night and got hard so I did what guys always do but I pulled my penis out by its roots and for some reason it stayed hard and I was able to finish what I started. I washed and dried it and put it into canister number two, still hard, only to be taken out and used at will.

A week later, after work, I stopped off for a couple of beers to wet my whistle and of course out popped my whistle. When I got home, Madge's car was in the driveway and I rushed to get out of the car and banged my knee which popped off and rolled down to the curb. I rinsed it off with the garden hose and went inside. Madge was in the kitchen wearing only an apron and setting the table with Chinese takeout. My thumb came off when I used the chop sticks to take some moo shoo pork and I asked her if she wouldn't mind washing it and patting it dry and putting it in canister number two. She did and found my penis and hustled me up to the bedroom where we had a great session. In the morning, I woke and Madge was gone and so was my penis. Frustrated for not thinking ahead, I slapped my forehead with my palm and both my palm and my forehead came off.

In despair, I shook my head.

Creeps

Apparently there are creeps everywhere. I hear my female co-workers talking about them over their cubicle walls. I sit on my bar stool, nursing my gin and tonic, staring straight ahead or doodling on a bar nap and listen to women at happy hour complaining about the creeps in their life. I don't know what makes a guy a creep. One of the four women next to me at the bar looked up and our eyes met in the back bar mirror. She motioned for her girlfriends to follow her and pointed to a table. "Creep," she said, passing behind me.

Lemon Pledge

"I forget why I'm telling you my innermost thoughts," I said to the shrink, Dr. Schmear.

"Because that's why you've come to see me," he said.

"No. I've come to see you because I haven't laughed since I was thirty-nine."

"Why thirty-nine and not forty or thirty-eight?" he asked.

"I was depressed the day I turned thirty-nine thinking that in another year I'd be forty and then fifty was right around the corner. And let's not forget," I said, "I'm paying you to help me find these answers—if I just give them to you I might as well stay home with my birds and eat Pop Tarts."

"What birds?" he asked.

"Petey, my parakeet and Kate Smith, my canary."

"Do you keep them in the same cage?"

"Would you put a dog and cat in the same cage?" I asked him. My chair arms were wood and had a greasy feel to them. I smelled my right arm then my left. They smelled like Lemon Pledge.

"That's an odd thing you just did," he said.

I was getting annoyed. I wanted out of his office.

I needn't have worried. Dr Schmear stood, walked over to the bookcase and removed a video-cam from between two books on 'The Zen of Masturbation'.

"I'll look at the films between now and your next appointment and I'll be able to tell a lot from your body language. We'll talk about it."

"Don't make me laugh," I said and opened the closet door thinking it was the hallway door. A woman in a nurse's uniform was standing behind a video camera on a tripod. She pointed to the exit door.

Cars, Trains and Smoke Rings

Harvey and me sat on the roof of his building in the projects. We had to shimmy up a tree to the branches and then use them ladder-like to get past the second floor and onto the flat asphalt roof. We watched the cars go by on the turnpike and talked. Sometimes a trucker would look our way and one or both of us would raise our hand and pull it down in a yanking movement and the trucker would do the same, blowing his air horn, and then we'd wave to each other.

The train tracks are between his building and the turnpike and we sometimes flatten pennies or bottle caps by laying them on the tracks. We do the whistle movement when the engineer looks our way and usually they blow their horn and wave and laugh since they're slowing down to pull into the Bridgeport station.

Harvey points to a man walking down the street towards the building we're on. "That's the Puerto Rican guy who just moved in. Him and his wife live two doors down from me. He comes home every day for lunch. My mother says he gets more than lunch."

Soon we hear Spanish voices from an open window and we scurry over and lay down atop the building in the area of their bedroom and lean over when Harvey tells me it's okay. The guy is on top of his wife humping away, her legs straight up in the air, and she's yelling in Spanish, and all the time her eyes are open and she's chewing gum looking at us looking at her. Finally she gives a yell and pounds his back with her fists and he collapses on her as she chews away.

He rolls off and grabs a cigarette from the pack on the floor and lights up, lies on his back and blows smoke rings as she turns her back to us and puts her arm over his chest. He looks at me and Harvey, our faces upside down, and blows a smoke ring in our direction and winks.

Code Red

When the bell rings and the color is announced, everyone not wearing the color of the day must stop what they are doing and sit, lie or lean. Today the color is green so the greens can go about their business—and at times their business is monkey business with greens of either sex.

The school is thinking of changing the rule, but today at the meeting to discuss it, the bell and "Code Green" come over the loudspeakers. The Assistant Dean and the English Lit teacher were in green so they exited via separate doors and met in their lover's alcove in a rarely used section of the building.

Since the Assistant Dean is often privy to the color of the day he makes the best of it.

A week after the meeting the rules have been modified. Now when the bell rings no one can talk. The people who get hurt the most are the ones having to get to a job or doctor's appointment so on the down low an insurgent group, The Anti-Colors, has been meeting and planning an overthrow of the school administration to do away with this tradition.

A week later the bell rings as everyone's settled in their home room and the announcements are made and the color "Yellow" is called out. The Anti-Colors ignore the bell and the loudspeaker and hurry to their assigned locations. First they take over the admin office and grab the microphone and announce, "As of today there will be no more bells and colors."

Two of the seniors, lying in wait, enter the Dean's office as he's about to enter the English Lit teacher who's bending over his desk, her yellow thong on the floor, his bright yellow sweater askew. He pulls his pants up and she gets off the desk and snags her thong and keeps it balled in her hand behind her back.

"We, as representatives of the students, demand you make an announcement agreeing with the abandonment of colors and bells." The Dean leaves the English Lit teacher and hurries over to the admin office and makes the announcement.

Students and teachers alike know he was forced into this position. They're expecting some kind of counter move and are at the ready.

For the first week everything is fine and then a fire breaks out in the back of the auditorium from faulty wiring and the announcement follows: "Code Red, Code Red, abandon the school immediately."

Code Red signifies danger and could be anything from a fire to a gunman but the students have wised up to their game-playing administration so they sit in their seats chatting away.

Honey & Darling

I hear them whispering to each other over dinner. My dining area backs to theirs and for some reason, in one small section of the wall I can hear everything. I found it by accident with one of the previous tenants. Perhaps when the building was built the insulation was left out or the builders did something intentionally to cause this.

It only works one way—them to me—I'm sure of that and would bet my life on it after living here through four other tenants.

He calls her Honey and she calls him Darling and their mailbox name slot is blank. They are cautious and only talk to each other in whispers. Obviously they must know that the walls in the building are thin but they can't know how thin in this one spot. I might as well be in their room with them. I keep my table next to the wall and eat my dinner when they have theirs, listening to them share their days' experiences and more.

I heard Honey tell Darling about a company that her company was about to buy so I bought stock and made several thousand dollars. She's the boss' secretary. Another time she told him about a stock that was about to tank and I shorted it and made even more. There have been others and I don't go crazy on these tips because I'm not greedy and don't want to bring suspicion down on my head. Besides, they keep coming.

Darling is a gangster. He lends money, breaks legs, pulls heists and worse. He tells Honey everything. I hope to write a gangster book one of these days so I keep my laptop on the table during dinner. At times I'm so busy listening and writing my meal gets cold.

At dinner this evening I listened as Darling said that he had to leave for a bit and take care of a problem. I have to squash a bug he said but I won't be long and I heard him push his chair back and walk to the door. I heard the squeak of it opening.

I heard a knock on my door.

Semantics

I walked into the grocery, grabbed a cart with all wheels working and went by the fruit and vegetables. I tried a red grape and then a green one and then I did the same with the organic which turned out to not look as good but to taste sweeter. I took a handful of the loose red organics from the bottom of the store bag and a plastic bag from the roll and left it on the kiddy seat to nibble on as I shopped. Some people think you have to buy the whole bag because that's the way it's packed. No way.

A lady was giving out samples of hummus on crackers and I don't particularly care for hummus and outright dislike the crackers they were using so I said no thank you and pushed my cart down the canned vegetable aisle and at the end there was a man heating chicken sausage slices in an electric frying pan and also putting them on crackers and together into small flimsy paper cups. I wouldn't eat chicken sausage unless the last two things on the planet to eat were spam and chicken sausage and the crackers were the same as the hummus crackers.

I was getting hungry and stopped at the deli counter and asked for two slices of boiled ham and then went over to the bakery department and took a roll from the bin using the tissue paper like they ask you to do. I made myself a sandwich with the boiled ham and newly acquired onion roll and felt full but thirsty so I wheeled over to the juice aisle and took one of the small V8s from the plastic gripper that holds six and washed down my sandwich.

A large man in a brown suit wearing a bright orange tie came over and asked what I was doing. Shopping, I said. He said he was the manager and watched me eating and drinking and I said, oh that, and he said, right that.

I was sampling, I told him. I didn't care for the store samples and wanted to choose my own.

That's not sampling, he said. That's pilfering.

Isn't pilfering just another word for sampling? I asked, and he said no, pilfering is another word for stealing.

I told him that we were just going to have to agree to disagree on this one and he said that's not how things work and he gave me the option of paying for my samples or leaving the store and not coming back unless I wanted him to get the police involved.

I told him that both his attitude and choice of samples leave a lot to be desired and I would just go ahead and leave his store and take my business elsewhere.

Good, he said, and I said good back to him.

Floaters

When you called, I let the phone ring three times and then picked it up. I was hoping you were calling to tell me you thought it over and we should try again and since we've had so many try agains we should be better at it this time but I only heard the dial tone and then I remembered you only give people two rings to answer your calls and, on the third ring the phone was on its way back to the cradle. We used to argue about your short window of answering opportunity and after a while I came to accept it, but truth is that sometimes it takes people more than two rings to cross the room and pick up their cell or their landline. We both know you're not going to change that quirk of yours and I know you hate when I call any of your quirks "quirks", but what else should I call them? I could call you back but you know the old salesman's rule—the first one that speaks loses and while you would be the first, technically by saying hello then I would have to speak more than one word and therefore would be on the losing end which might not be so bad if it got us back together or at least to a coffee shop or a motel or a play-out of one of our fantasies. You've been in my fantasies lately in a strange way. I started thinking I saw mice running across the floorboards by the TV and I'd look away from my book and I'd never catch the little bastards. Then that morphed into my seeing birds flying by up high while I was driving, and this went on for a couple of weeks and then the mice came back and no, I'm not doing any drugs, but I started worrying about my eyes and I went to see the ophthalmologist and he told me I had "floaters" and it's not a big deal and I told him I didn't want floaters and he said many people get them and I'd get used to them and they're not worth operating on and I don't want my eyes operated on anyway but I don't want floaters either. The doctor told me that it's an age-related thing where the jelly-like substance in my eyes becomes more liquid. I asked him if he had jelly drops I could add and he laughed and called his associates in to ask them in front of me about the jelly drops and they all had a good laugh at my expense and so I left and the birds were gone and that evening the mice were gone but later that day, in the upper part of my eye you were floating by, only you were in a line with other Rockettes, high kicking with arms on each others' shoulders as you went from left to right and all the Rockettes had your face and you were all wearing skimpy costumes and I kind of liked seeing you floating by all sexy and smiling and I knew that must have meant you were thinking of me and then you called so I'm returning your call to see how you're doing and if you think we ought to move back into the "try again" mode and—oh, your lawyer wants my lawyer's name well I don't have a lawyer and why because you've been seeing someone and you're getting kind of serious well I'm happy for you but don't forget about floaters cause this character might only be floating on by and then what? You know what I mean?

This Has Got to Stop

Manny's right hand was out of control. It swung wildly, punching him in his left shoulder, forearm and then bloodying his nose with two more ferocious roundhouses. Meanwhile Manny's left hand played with the change in his pocket.

Righty finally tired himself out, and Lefty, no longer tossing the loose change, was now playing pocket pool. Righty reached around to get the handkerchief and held it up to Manny's nose to help stem the flow of blood.

Lefty, having just gotten off, took his hand out of his pocket and took charge of the handkerchief. He wiped his hand and Manny's nose simultaneously while Righty shook, trying to get the soreness out.

Manny sat down on the curb trying to figure out what he'd done to Righty this time. Righty, for his part, hoped that Manny learned his lesson but just in case he hadn't, Righty lifted Manny's right leg and with his size twelve Doc Martins stomped on Lefty's ankle, knocking Manny back screaming. He was lying on the sidewalk wailing like a baby when a cop car drove up and two gorilla-sized cops got out, ran over and asked Manny what happened.

One helped lift Manny to a sitting position while the other called an ambulance. Putting away his cell phone he asked, "Who did this to you?" and Manny looked around and saw his wife's brother pull into their driveway and pointed his sore right finger at him. Both cops took off after him, tackling him before he got to the front door and knocking his ultra-suede skullcap off.

Changing of the Guard

Lawrence "Lucky Larry" Lombardi, 62, loving husband of Mary Lombardi for forty years passed suddenly while hooking up a new tank to his beloved eight burner gas grill. Besides his wife he leaves behind brothers Jimmy and Tommy and their wives and five nieces and nephews. He was active in Little League, girls soccer, Meals on Wheels, The Elks Club, The Polar Bear Club and an advocate for the homeless. Lucky Larry loved life, the New York Yankees and the Giants and his poker nights. He was the proprietor of Lucky Larry's Package Store for over thirty years and made hundreds of friends, one of which, Timmy Nolan, will be buying the store. Out of respect and love for Larry he will be keeping the name.

Timmy will be doubling the wine section and naming it Lucky's Wine Cove and promises that he will give the same fine service that Larry did over the years and will be keeping the same schedule. For his first month he wants to honor Larry by giving a 10% discount on all beer, wine and liquor (excluding pints and half pints). He is also instituting a delivery service. In addition, in keeping up with the times, you'll be able to fax or email your order and have it waiting at the new drive through window he's installing. Beginning in two weeks there will be wine and bourbon tastings and a weekly drawing for a bottle of Tito's Vodka. "My goal is to do Larry proud," Timmy says.

Larry will also be deeply missed by his weekly poker game buddies, Tony L., Tony M., Skinny Joe, and Salami Sal and the Horowitz brothers, Herb and Murray.

Services for Larry will be at Our Lady of Perpetual Agony Church at 10am Saturday with calling hours from 5-7 Thursday and Friday. (Timmy Nolan will be closing Lucky Larry's during funeral hours and will re-open at 1pm for a "Have a glass of beer for Larry" memorial.)

In lieu of flowers, contributions may be made to The Mary Lombardi Mason Jar Fund.

The Only Hope
of the Jews

You're sitting on your stoop thinking how much you hate the stoop, the building you live in with six side-by-side apartments (now called town houses) and the neighborhood. You hate the neighborhood because all of the stoops in all of the buildings and all of the wire-fenced in tiny yards smaller than a jail cell look alike and your fourteen-year-old self can't wait to get out of these projects and scrub the stigma off and live in a place where you don't need the roach exterminator every month and head lice are the main pets for the little kids and on top of it all your family are the only Jews in all the buildings. There are lots of blacks and Puerto Ricans (who are mortal enemies) and plenty of white people and there's a big Catholic Church on the corner across from the corner store with its two pinballs and playing those pinballs is your only solace here. You look to your left and you see a couple of older and bigger kids coming down the walk and you reach behind you and grab the rock that you scraped against the cement stoop to make jagged edges that makes your fist a weapon and you don't care how big or how many Jew-haters there are you will go after them. Rock in hand you'll punch them repeatedly until they subdue you and "teach you a lesson". You know you'll never learn your lesson and when your mother comes home she'll take one look at you and punish you for fighting and you'll never tell her you're the only hope of the Jews and she thinks you've gotten to be a ruffian since you had to move to this neighborhood and that unlike your brother and sisters you're hanging out with the wrong crowd. You take your punishment from her and dream of owning a car and driving as far away from that stoop as you can and never having to carry a jagged rock in your pocket again.

Father Panik Village

Father Panik Village in Bridgeport, Connecticut, the worst of the worst in the failed projects experiment, was scheduled to be demolished and I wanted to see my old neighborhood one last time. We lived here until there was a vacancy in a better project, Marina Village.

Across the street the once busy factories were closed, their razor-wired factory fences wrapped along the two desolate blocks. Large For Sale signs were nailed to the buildings.

The police had stopped patrolling it on a regular basis years earlier for fear of getting shot. Now, windows of the vacant units were boarded, graffiti was everywhere. The parking lot where we shot craps or played black jack was now littered with abandoned cars and broken glass.

Yet the people who were being made to move protested about being thrown out of the only house some had ever known. In place of the ninety apartments, the city was going to build ten small houses that would go by lottery to dispossessed families.

I drove the parameter and then cut through the side streets looking for the last time at the ugliness of these three-story brick buildings once vibrant with kids playing and the aged and unemployed sitting around smoking and playing tonk for pennies. Good memories and bad.

I saw a young girl leaning against a building and I pulled to the curb. "Hi. You've got to be the last person in Panik."

I offered her a stick of gum. She took two and said, "One's for later."

"How come you're still here? What are you fifteen, sixteen?"

"Fourteen and my man told me to stay here till he calls for me."

"How long ago was that?"

"Couple of days."

"Hungry?"

Her look said yes.

"C'mon. We'll go to the Hot Top Diner and get a good meal. Have you back in no time."

"He'll be at the diner. I'd like a Happy Meal."

She walked to my car and got in.

"Ella," she said.

"Pretty name."

"My momma liked Ella Fitzgerald."

"I'm Ben," I said.

We went through the drive-through and Ella didn't order a Happy Meal. She asked if she could order extra for later and I said sure and she ordered enough for three grown-ups and ate fries all the way to the Seaside Park. I stopped the car facing the water and took out my own small bag of fries and a Coke.

"Do you live with your parents?" I asked her.

She didn't answer.

"Where are you going to go when they bulldoze Panik?"

She shrugged and that's how our meal went. I told her there were places that would take her in and send her to school. Places that were clean and she'd have friends and her own room but she didn't respond.

Finally, she folded her bag and put it on the floor. "That was good, Mr. Ben, I still have enough for a good meal tonight." I started the car. Ella slurped the last of her Coke and reached over and put her hand on my crotch, grabbing the zipper with practiced hands.

I pushed her hands away. "Put your seat belt on," I said.

She began to unbutton her blouse.

"Button up, I'm not interested."

Ella pouted on the drive until we reached Panik and I stopped the car. "Here's my phone number." I gave her a business card. "Call me if you want to go to one of those nice places I told you about."

"Listen," she said. "Gimme twenty dollars or he'll be angry. Please."

I gave her two tens and she opened the car door. "Don't forget your food," I said and she took the bags and ran. I watched her hold them out as an offering and drove off; my business card lying where Ella sat minutes ago.

Mirsky's Rebellion

"Try to understand the reason for my moving out," Mirsky told Elaine, his wife of 46 years.

"All you're taking with you is this box of books and some energy bars? That doesn't make sense," Elaine said.

"Sure it does. I'll come home to eat, shower and change clothes."

"And you expect me to continue to cook for you and wash your clothes?"

"Why not? You've got to cook for yourself and do your own wash. Why exclude me?"

"Why are you excluding me?"

"I'm not. I'll see you at meal times and for bathroom breaks and you can occasionally visit me."

"And what about bad weather?"

"You'll probably see me during bad weather also. I want to enjoy my time in the backyard tent reading and roughing it; but roughing it has its limits."

"So do I."

Mother of the Bride

Betsy, home from the gym, left her car in the garage and walked back up the driveway to the mailbox. Along with the flyers and other mail was a large wedding invitation-sized envelope with her daughter, Terri's, return address. Terri hadn't spoken to her in over a year despite Betsy's many attempts to re-establish contact.

But now, with a joyous heart, she planned to open her invitation with her morning coffee after showering. She was anxious but pushed herself to stretch out her upcoming pleasure and ruminate on it for a bit.

Betsy raced through her shower, dressed and went to the kitchen. Skipping her coffee she opened the envelope. It was an invitation to Terri's wedding alright, but in every conceivable place was written in **NOT**. *You are* **Not** *invited to the wedding of Terri and . . .*

The return card was filled out for her. *I will* **Not** *be attending. . .*

The meal choice was filled with a dash as was the brunch the next day.

Written at the bottom of the non-invitation invitation was a note: *Please read the letter that came in the same day's mail for an explanation. T*

That letter remained unopened on Betsy's counter for so many days that she no longer saw it—like a pair of socks on the stairs waiting to be carried up to the laundry, they just become a part of the landscape after a while.

The following month, on the day of the wedding, Betsy opened a bottle of wine and poured herself a glass; her first in over three years of sobriety and sat down with the letter she knew would hurt her even more.

Betsy was more than half way through the bottle when she finally had the courage to open the letter. She poured one more full glass and read:

Mom, I sent you that invitation so you can feel some of the hurt you have unleashed on me over the years. Your years of drinking and the embarrassment and humiliation it's caused me personally and professionally has made me your bitter angry child. But now I've decided to forgive you and I want you to know how proud of you I am for sticking with your sober life. I want you at my wedding to walk me down the aisle. It will mean so much to the both of us—I just know it. I love you. Your loving daughter, Terri.

Betsy was crying by the time she finished the letter and looked over at the clock. It was blurry and she couldn't make out the time but she knew that her daughter needed her so she got up and staggered to her bedroom to find something to wear that would pass as a mother-of-the-bride dress and hurried to the hall where the wedding was taking place.

Unfortunately, she made it in time, driving drunk, fast and erratically without the good fortune of being pulled over and arrested, as she had so often in her past.

Finding Grandma Pearl

We went with Mom and Dad to help clean out Grandma's house after she died. It was Mom's mother and even though she was ninety-four we weren't ready to say goodbye.

Mom insisted we wait for a couple of weeks. She had girls cleaning out the bedrooms and separating things and she sent me and Mark up to the hot, dingy attic to work there. The place was loaded with trunks and was very neat. We opened up the first trunk and, sitting atop the folded clothes and books, was a diary.

It was more of a listing than a diary or a combination of both and it started the night before her wedding when she had sex with her cousin Harry and later that night when she shared a room with cousin Betsy and they got it on also.

Grandma was not a prude. She took on all comers in the sack. Mark and I got through half her diary when Mom yelled that she was coming up so we hid the diary and opened another trunk and pulled out clothes and tossed them around.

Mom decided we weren't working hard enough so she stayed with us and finally we came to a trunk of books all written by someone we'd never heard of but the paperback covers were sexy enough to make me and Mark blush.

Mom said, "Grandma supported her family writing. She wrote for men's magazines, bodice ripper paperbacks and anything that would pay and keep the family together.

Strange because Mom was a prude but was somehow able to come up with romantic and sexy scenes that people wanted to read. She used two pen names, A.J. Fingersmith and Thurgood M. DuPont."

"I don't know where Grandma got her fertile imagination from to write this stuff," Mom said, and with that I eased her diary into my backpack.

Fantasy Party

She led me down a dark dirt path. I'd met her fifteen minutes into the party, we talked for maybe ten minutes, and she said, *let's blow this Popsicle stand*, and I, always ready to follow a redhead, agreed. Our only light was the flash from her iPhone and we ended up at an old barn. "This is what I wanted to show you," she said, sliding the barn door open and heading towards a far corner. "That was the path to the nest of spiders." She began to undress and said, "Nothing turns me on more than making love in the straw, knowing there are spiders only inches away."

I will only follow a redhead so far and said adios and I found my way back to the fantasy party where I re-introduced myself to the bartender and chugged a double bourbon with one cube to settle me down. I saw the redhead again and watched her lead someone else out towards the path.

"If I had a drink like you just did, I'd feel like my soul's on fire," a safer and more hopefully sane brunette said. "Don't much like spiders?"

"Not much," I said, feeling the bourbon mellow and massage my insides.

She said, "Let's grab another drink and go down by the swings. I've never gotten over my love of playground swings. I love Bill's parties, don't you?" I told her I'd never been to one before and she said, "wrong answer," and then I remembered the invite rules: make everything up including your name, occupation and phone number. This is my first annual Fantasy Party, the invitation read.

It was a pleasant evening and, truth be told, it was fun swinging and sipping my drink. "Want me to push you," I asked and she said, "Maybe after we get to know each other better and by the way, what's your name?"

"Arnold," I said.

"That's the name of my accountant, gynecologist and former divorce lawyer and also the name the Indian man uses when he calls to sell me solar panels. My name's Henrietta and after the spider episode what gave you the courage to follow me outside?"

"Cleavage," I said and she said, "You realize you said that aloud, don't you?"

"The bourbon is the key that unlocks the filter between my brain and mouth," I said and Henrietta said she found that charming. Then she said, "Okay, you can push me now," and I stopped my swing and pulled the ropes on hers back and pushed her forward.

She kept saying higher, higher, which my brain heard as harder harder so I pulled back and let it rip and pushed her harder and higher and when she was above the top of the swing, she let go of the ropes and spread her arms and flew off to parts unknown. I walked back to the party, thinking perhaps I wasn't cut out for Fantasy Parties and went to the bar where the bartender was ready with my double bourbon and one cube. I looked around and saw the spider lady and the swing lady entwined on the couch and walked out, glass in hand, looking for a cab.

A Great Multi-Tasker

"There is no way to fix what's broken. Don't you understand?"

"But I'm a good man, a good provider."

"That doesn't mean that you have to provide for three different families in three different states. That doesn't make you a good man—it makes you a bigamist, a criminal, a liar and a cheat. You deprived our children and me time you could have been spending with us."

"You never complained about lack of time or attention before. I'm a great multi-tasker—you've got to admit that. Listen. All I ask is that you go through with the get-together before you make a final decision. You ladies could be sisters and the eight kids are already half siblings. What's the harm in meeting? It's a beautiful day for a picnic and I've taken care of ordering and delivery. All of the gluten and peanut allergies have been taken into consideration. I've thought of everything."

"You think so, do you? Do you realize we're Jewish and not Mormon?"

"All my wives are Jewish. What makes you think I'd marry out of the faith?"

Spice of Life

Smell this, my husband said, holding out a wooden spoon with red sauce. I looked at him quizzically and he looked back at me the same way.

Smell, he said.

Stare, I did.

He moved the spoon closer to my nose. This is going to be my best sauce ever, he said. Smell.

What could I do? I smelled.

Well? He waited.

I nodded.

Satisfied, he left the sauce simmering on the stove and went into the living room to watch sports.

I added spices, stirred them in and tasted.

At dinner he was so proud of his sauce that he gave me a good poking that night.

Gardenville

There were only mothers and only single mothers: women abandoned, never married, divorced mothers sent here by the court because they were considered "at risk" mothers. There were other single parent mothers who wanted in to what was considered "the best" of Garden View Village nicknamed Gardenville, but they were not allowed into this section, in the center of the Projects. They never understood why the good mothers lived on the outskirts in the original smaller apartments, in buildings that were all in disrepair, while the evils lived in the safety of the three-story brick buildings with flat roofs, small dirt yards with clothes lines.

There was an office in Gardenville's Building One that held four government surplus metal desks, file cabinets and mismatched chairs for the social workers. There was one for the guard. There were also three doors, always closed. Behind the first, a room of beds. The second held an infirmary and the third housed cells.

All the mothers in Gardenville were child beaters, welfare cheats, women who looked up to trailer trash and bullies (both physical and psychological). They not only beat their kids but the fathers of their children, the teachers, school bus drivers and each other on a regular basis.

By being allowed into Gardenville, instead of jail, they were required to get their GEDs if needed, and to go to anger management courses every day, which only made them angrier.

These mothers had one major thing in common—they all blamed their kids for their plight in this world, which is why they withheld food, clean clothes, and any kind of affection. The worst of the mothers ended up in cells behind door number three, while their kids were fostered out to surrogate mothers from Gardenville who supposedly had their issues under control and were but a step away from being monitored and dangerous. But, none-the-less, the infirmary was kept open and busy 24/7 for children in the complex.

After the second boy went missing, people started talking and speculating on which Gardenville mother was the culprit. Of course, the mothers of the two boys were the prime suspects but they both happened to be in cells behind door number three. The guards were ordered to patrol instead of sitting in their office and the social workers were all questioned.

When nine-year-old Theresa disappeared, the gossip mongers got to work but the only people not upset were the mothers of Gardenville. The state police were called in to help locate the missing children and the only people not interrogated were the good mothers who couldn't get into Gardenville.

After a year, half the children were missing, and a good number of Gardenville mothers who no longer had a reason to live there moved out. Word was that when Gardenville became childless all the apartments would become available.

One of three social workers poking around a newly vacated apartment spotted the linoleum lifted up in one corner, peeled it back, and found the entrance to a tunnel. She grabbed her flashlight and followed the tunnel to see where it came out, but kept silent after returning to the apartment and gluing the linoleum back into place.

Columbia Market

I stood next to Burt, his Old Spice scent filling my nostrils as I watched him saw two steaks coated with mold and then had me bring the rest of the beef back into the cooler and put it on a hook. It was a heavy load for a thirteen-year-old kid. Once back out he was scraping the mold off the steaks into the barrel filled with fat that would be going to the fat renderer on Friday.

"Nothing is as tender as these steaks will be," he said. "Maybe I'll call you upstairs and let you taste a piece."

He told me to scrub the block. I held the wood brush with the solid metal teeth and pushed back and forth until there was no more sign of blood or meat on the butcher block which was worn down in the middle from years of metal brush cleaning.

Burt and Betty had an apartment in the back and the kitchen overlooked the entrance and a good part of the narrow store.

"Bring me up garlic and a small onion," he yelled down and I did and saw that the table was set for two with nice China and two glasses of white wine. The steaks were in a fry pan on the gas range and Burt said, "All you need to cook these perfect is salt on the pan bottom, and then top it off with butter, grilled onions and garlic. Smells incredible, doesn't it?"

I heard the bell and walked down to the store and sold a loaf of Wonder Bread, a pack of Pall Malls and the lady wanted two pork chops. I went into the cooler, took out the rack and sliced two down to the bone and then with the cleaver, chopped through for two one inch thick chops and weighed them atop a piece of butcher paper. She watched to see that I didn't have my thumb on the scale and I didn't—I had it on the draped butcher paper adding about twenty-five cents to her chops. She added a can of green beans to her order and I added it up on her paper bag and then wrote it on her running tab.

She left and I returned the rack to the cooler, scrubbed the butcher block down again and went out from behind the counter where Burt and Betty could see me and straightened some cans and then began sweeping the floor.

"Reuven, come up here before the steak is all gone."

I didn't want their lousy steak but I was hungry and weak-willed so I climbed the stairs to their apartment and Burt cut off a nickel sized piece of steak and said, "Try a piece of the best." I chewed it and made the right mm mmm sounds and wanted to run down and make myself a bologna sandwich I was so hungry. "Next time I'll cut a bigger piece so you can have more," he said.

The phone rang and Betty got up to take the call and I went back downstairs, trying to figure out what I could steal and get away with, when Betty called me back. "That was your mother—she wants you to bring three hot dogs and a can of vegetarian beans home for supper tonight."

I only lived around the corner in the projects and we ate mostly casseroles because that's what my mother could afford, supporting three boys. I weighed the hot dogs and put their exact weight and cost along with the beans on my mother's tab.

I loaded the garbage can of fat back into the cooler after reaching up and taking the fat from the corner of the chopped meat tray. We always added some extra fat to the chuck steak when someone wanted hamburger. I swept behind the counter and Burt and Betty came down. Burt checked my mother's bag and her tab and Betty gave me her nightly hug and told me to go home to my family. She thought she was making me feel cared for with the hug but I knew she was really frisking me.

Mom on the USO Circuit

My mother likes to tell the story about the time she met Elvis in Germany. She said she almost didn't recognize him because he had a military crew cut and no pompadour but as soon as he began their duet, 'Bi Mir Bist du Schein', she was so taken aback he had to start over so she could jump in.

My mother's never been to Germany and she won't eat sauerkraut or drive in a VW Beetle because of WWII. Yet, she insists he gave her a box of chocolates, a Whitman Sampler two pounder, after the show. But she says that hip gyrating playboy asked her out to a schnitzel buffet but she turned him down because she heard the Priscilla rumors—everyone did she said and she wasn't about to play second fiddle for Elvis anymore than she would have for Bing when he came calling.

Because of her sexy voice and body she was the object of her fellow USO members' desires but as she told us years later, she saved herself for that slick bucket salesman from New York who, with the aid of a fake quarter carat diamond ring, swept her off her feet and away from the stage to the thrill of a cold water flat on the Lower East Side. When they returned from their honeymoon at Busters in the Catskills and he carried her over the threshold, her first instinct was to box his ears and run back to showbiz but he had a way about him. Plus, she was in a family way.

Life went downhill from there. Dad lost his bucket territory and opened a pickle stand on Delancy, but my mother turned out to be allergic to the spices in pickles and thus to my father so, now expecting her second child, they divorced and she got in vaudeville right at the tail end and was an understudy for Gracie Allen who thankfully was a hypochondriac so Mom had a fairly steady income until she got pregnant again and she swears that the boy came out looking like George Burns, cigar and all.

Her showbiz career was over so we moved in with her parents in their two-bedroom third floor flat where her sister Dee was living with her husband and baby. Mom got a job as a torch singer in the Flamingo Club and Aunt Dee raised us when Mom left there to go on the circuit once again after Elvis tracked her down to be one of his backup singers.

There are no pictures of her showbiz career and no one in the family will talk about it so while Mom, whose brain is addled from reefer and gin, mumbles out her stories, we kids think of her as our crazy aunt and our Aunt Dee as our mother. And strangely enough, Mom can't carry a tune in a big red bucket.

That seems to work for everyone so let's let it lie.

Dean's Dilemma

My friend Dean has no eyebrows. He has a full head of curly hair, has to shave, has some chest hair but never got the eyebrow gene. It wouldn't be so bad if he was a plumber, an architect or a gynecologist but he's my dentist and I feel I have a cartoon character as my dentist staring down at me with his eyebrowless face every six months.

For his tenth anniversary in practice I organized a group of his patient friends to chip in and get him a gift certificate for eyebrow plugs.

"What the hell do I need eyebrows for? What function do they serve?"

Feeling the pressure from his friends he made an appointment and went, but returned with eyebrows drawn on and a recommendation that he have them tattooed instead of plugs.

"You're a Jew and Jews don't believe in tattoos unless you're Adam Levine," I told him.

Trying to make light of the subject and delaying the whole plug deal, Dean let his wife draw eyebrows on in different colors and sizes such as red, white and blue for Independence Day, blue and yellow for Chanukah and of course, green and red for Christmas.

One St. Patty's Day, four couples went out for corned beef and cabbage and green beers or green Grey Goose Martinis. Dean went over his limit. His emerald green eyebrows drooped around his half mast eyes and he slapped the table and said, "I have an announcement: I'm having the eyebrow plugs put in next week."

He expected something so we gave him a round of applause and he stood on a chair and took a bow and then dropped trow and mooned us. "Did you notice there wasn't a hair on my ash?" he slurred. "They're waiting for me to come in and have them used as plugs. I've been going to New York every week to have some removed and stored waiting for the right time and that time is next week."

As much as we cared for Dean, it was going to be a struggle looking at his ass hairs hanging above his eyes. He had no idea what he was in for when asked about his new eyebrows by patients not in on the down low.

I Am Not
the Marathon Man

I remember the pinch of the needle going into my arm and feeling myself relax as the Versed entered in and the fear of pain ebbed away. There was to be no pain for the four hours. I was promised no pain and yet the pain was endless. I lifted my hand for a break from what I thought were needles going deep and non-stop.

Put your hand down the dentist said and I tried to tell him I needed a short break but I knew my words were noise to him. They were incoherent to me. Hand down, he said again and again.

I went out and again I raised my hand when the pain woke me and once again, he sharply told me to put my hand down and I went off into space until once again the pain, the harsh pain, the non-stop pain, the pain, the pain, and I raised my hand, not like over my head, to answer a question in school, but from the arm of the chair, the universal signal to stop that even in my drugged world I knew—only my hand didn't raise, couldn't lift, and I knew if it didn't raise he wouldn't know I needed a respite and for the first time and the only time since I sat in his chair I opened my eyes and looked down at my hand and saw my arm bound to the armrest with brown rope—a thick brown twisted rough rope and I saw it around my leg and I went limp thinking about

Mengele, fucking Mengele, and how I wanted to hurt this man looming over me, hurting me, but I had no power so I collapsed into his chair, giving in.

Columbia Market Delivers

While Burt waited in the truck I started up the back stairs with the box of groceries I was to leave in the kitchen. The third step squeaked and I froze and could smell my fear mixed with sweat. I saw a light through the balustrades and peeked in the open door and saw a fat, naked man lying on a metal table. His death smell rose like heat and it hit me and I ran up the stairs to the apartment over the funeral parlor and without knocking I opened the door to the kitchen and put the groceries on the counter and headed back for the other box.

A stream of smoke cut off my exit and the man behind it asked if I happened to see a fat, naked, dead man, on the way up. I starred at Mr. Dichello and he smiled and asked again, said he misplaced him and the smile showed his two gold teeth, one above the other, shining bright from the overhead light.

"I'm going down for your other groceries," I said.

"Where's Burt?" he asked.

"He's in the truck waiting for me so I'd better hurry."

"Well, if you see that naked, fat, dead man hold onto him and give me a yell, willya?"

I tasted the Devil Dog come up in my throat. I'd swiped it from the store and ate it quick before Bert came down with the order. "Get two boxes and I'll call out the items. You bring them over and I'll pack 'em up and you can come with me to Dichello's to deliver them."

I ran down the stairs and didn't look back at the fat, naked, dead guy on the table and was sweating and shaking when I got to the truck.

"You look like you've seen a ghost," Burt laughed. "Bring this other box up quick so we can deliver the rest of the groceries."

As soon as the back door closed behind me I stuck my head in the box and breathed in the fresh seeded rye bread. I sucked in the smell afraid I'd suck the seeds out. Finally, I lifted my head and took the stairs two at a time barely glimpsing the naked, fat, dead man's feet.

Goodbye Already

They were sitting around a fire pit talking and chewing pepperoni sticks and eating bruschetta when I walked into my cousin's back yard in Lucca, the great walled city in Tuscany. We had been out walking the wall, people watching and catching up with family stories and horrors. I knew nothing of most of them but he was familiar with my New York branch of the family.

I saw the dead family members whose funerals I hadn't been to over the years. My cousin gave me names and family connections. They were chatting away and there were women in maid's uniforms taking orders and bringing out appetizers and drinks. The big deal was the pigs in a blanket (the pigs being kosher of course) and shrimp—they couldn't bring out the 12-15 size shrimp fast enough and there was a raw bar with clams and oysters.

A bell tolled and all the dead materialized over at picnic tables for the main course and dessert. They only spoke to the servers and not each other anymore. There was a pasta station and a porchetta cutting station, a mac and cheese station and a dessert station with cannolis, panna cotta, sfogliatelle and gelato. I noticed people putting food in their napkins, like in the old days, for a late-night snack or breakfast.

I sat on the back steps watching and smoking unfiltered Camels one after another and stopped one of the servers and asked for a drink and was told sorry, you're not on the guest list so I went inside my cousin's house where I was staying and poured myself four fingers of nasty grappa and went and sat down again, but decided to leave when the accordion player and the harmonica group showed up.

Another Day at the Office

Voice tells me it's all been solved but I'm not willing to take Voice at face value. In the past Voice gave me a sure thing on a trifecta and it cost my Lexus to pay the book. Voice also misled me on Diana, a co-worker who was supposedly interested in me. I followed her into the supply room and told her how sexy she was and she went straight to HR.

Diana's been promoted to vice-president and I report directly to her. Her second day in her new office she messaged me to show up at one, which is my lunchtime, so I had to decide if I was going to walk into her office eating my pastrami (lean) on rye or walk in hungry. I chose hungry.

Her door was open so I went in and sat. She eventually showed up eating an egg salad on white bread, mayo oozing out the sides of the sandwich and her mouth. "My lunch is at one and I had to grab something. Sorry to keep you waiting."

I started to apologize and she told me to forget it—my instincts were right but she had to set some rules knowing she was getting promoted. She proposed a friends with benefits deal. "Who knows, it might even help your career."

I was too mesmerized watching mayo run down towards her neck to answer and since I hate the taste and smell of egg salad I prayed she didn't want to start right away.

Chica Radar

Mirsky lies on his lounge chair, book resting on his stomach, hiding as best he can from the sun under a low hanging bough. He had begun reading the same paragraph innumerable times, only to be pulled away by the poolside activities. He closes his book, places it on the ground and changes his reading glasses for dark sunglasses, which allow him to watch the action without appearing to be staring.

He has come to Cuba to reflect on his marriage to Elaine. She went off with her girlfriends to a lake in Vermont. Their Connecticut house rests peacefully in their absence.

The pool at the Hotel Nacional is huge. Many scenarios play out in and around it. Mirsky watches a couple, young lovers, standing in chest high water cuddling. They kiss and rub each other as if they were alone in their room. Their bodies shine as one in the summer sun. Several men with arms folded, resting atop their bellies, stand in the shallow end talking, separated only by their guts and their unlit Monte Christos.

Waiters walk by with Daiquiris, Mohitos and bottles of Cristol Beer. They pass again with fat Cuban sandwiches, hamburgers and fries. Not ten feet away from Mirsky a waiter places an order on a table and the three women, girls really, reach for their drinks. The one who is reclining in her lounger has to snub out her cigarette first and lift her head to take a sip, while her boyfriend lies stretched out between her legs with his cheek on her round brown belly. She rubs his head in a circular motion and he turns his face and kisses her belly, his right hand caressing her left breast through her halter-top.

Her girlfriends chat while she stares off into the distance, and her little son, maybe four years old, runs back and forth between his mother and the pool. All the while this young man, and he is younger than this barely out of her teens mother, never stops doing what he's been doing. His chest is slowly moving over her mons as he continues kissing her stomach, licking in and around her navel. And she never breaks stride from her food or smoke except finally for a brief flurry of thrashes and thrusts as she pushes her free hand down on his back. He squirms even more atop her.

Her girlfriends smile and the young man stays where he is and turns his cheek onto her belly and appears to doze off. She takes a bite of her Cuban sandwich and then holds it out to her son.

Across the pool, Mirsky watches a man unbutton a woman's blouse. She aids him by shaking it free from her large breasts that now sway uninhibited. He holds her bikini top out to her, but before putting it on she spends a couple of minutes rubbing suntan oil on her chest, as their three kids stand around getting the lay of the land. Finally, with her breasts gleaming in the sun, she lets her man slip the top on to cover them. Her husband and children run and dive into the pool as she lies down on the lounge chair. Mirsky watches her roll over, face down, and bring her hands up behind her back unhooking her top, the falling straps exposing her once again. It causes him to think of Elaine on the nude beach in St. John. She was lying down reading, her elbows pushing her up off the sand, while he looked at her boobs, remembering the pleasure they had given him only hours before. He wished she were here now; not today's Elaine, but the one from the St. John days.

Two chicas have approached Mirsky at poolside. The first one asking if he'd like to buy her a Coca-Cola and minutes later the other asking if he'd like company for lunch. Both are young and wear skimpy bathing suits that are purposely too small. He declines both with a shake of his head. Their smiles let him know that they didn't take his rejections personally.

Chicas aren't expected to be at the pool anymore than the other locals enjoying the day there. Mirsky had seen a sign by the towel boy explaining that the pool is open to anyone— free to hotel guests but a $5 charge for others. For most that is more than a week's salary and enough to keep the pool almost exclusively upper class and tourist.

Mirsky, after looking around and thinking about the sign, sees things differently. He compares the locals visiting the Hotel National pool to one of his extravagant nights out with Elaine. Yesterday, at the beach he watched a group of teens sharing a massive amount of food brought from home, but here they keep the waiters busy bringing food and drink.

Mirsky turns his attention back to the young lovers in the pool. Her arms are wrapped around his neck, their bodies melding into one as they kiss long passionate kisses. Kids swim by ignoring them, interested only in their own agendas. They don't see what Mirsky does, her pink bikini top draped over the pool edge.

Mirsky realizes that he's hard. Neither his trunks nor the towel draped across his lap hide the product of his thoughts. One of the chicas gets up and begins her stroll around the pool, never taking her eyes from him or pretending otherwise. She walks slowly but purposefully. Chica radar, Mirsky muses, trying to remember if she's the Coca Cola chica or the lunch chica; not that it really matters anymore.

Betty's Live Chat Help Line

Betty: Our next texter is standing by and wants to be known as Anonymous. What's your issue, Anonymous?

Anonymous: She's got an attitude and I've finally had enough. I'm so annoyed I won't even speak her name and I told her so and she came right back with a snide remark.

Betty: What did she say that was snide?

A: She said, Well I wouldn't want my clean name in your dirty mouth.

B: You have to admit that was a good one.

A: Not so good to me. A couple of days earlier I asked her— As long as you're up will you please bring me a glass of water? Are your legs broken? Get up and get it yourself, she said.

B: Do you think she had a point?

A: How is this remark justified? She claims that I'm the one with the attitude and I've got to learn a lesson or life is going to be difficult. This is difficult. Living with her comebacks and putdowns is difficult.

Last night I asked her—What are we having for dinner? Stay where you are—I'll bring you a menu as soon as I finish printing it up, she says. Why couldn't she just answer a simple question?

B: Have you thought of a trial separation? Maybe you two need to be apart for a bit to appreciate each other.

A: How does a thirteen-year-old boy go about getting a trial separation from his mother?

Commuter

I now know if I take the 7am subway I'm liable to get groped, whereas, if I take the 6pm train back I'm almost certain to be groped. I discuss this with my new shrink. Her solution is quite simple and clear: Don't take either of these. They come often enough so a half hour either way shouldn't make a difference in your life. Obviously, she's forgotten my reason for seeing her. There are times a woman needs the intimate touch of another person. I think I'll cancel my future appointments since I've now figured it out for myself.

A Visit from Grammy

"I play to win so don't fuck with me," Grammy Esta said as she dealt out a hand of gin.

I was fourteen and just met her for the first time and didn't know how to take her. She was young for a grandmother and looked the same age as my friends' mothers.

"Two cents a point to a hundred and double for a schneid. Got it?"

"I have to go to my room and get my piggy bank. I don't carry money around unless I'm going to the mall."

"Go ahead and get your piggy bank and think of this experience as going to the mall with Grammy."

Grammy won all the money in my piggy bank and then she won my piggy bank on a schneid.

The next night, while Mom was working, Grammy showed me how to play five card stud and since I didn't have any money left she gave me my choice of washing her car or her hair. I chose the car.

Mom was off work the next two nights and we went out for dinner one night and to the movies the next.

That next night I learned backgammon. Boy did I learn. Grammy creamed me and gave me a break from having to pay off on any bet. I did win two games though.

"Ever hear of strip poker?" she asked the following night when we were driving back from Burger King.

"Kinda," I said, "but I've never played it."

"Well, sonny, after tonight you won't be able to say that again."

I was down to just my tighty-whities and Grammy had only her bra and panties. "I need a beer for the next hand," she said. "Want one?"

"You bet!"

Grammy had just dealt me a pat hand—three fours and a pair of queens—a full house and I was sitting all smug-like, sipping on my beer and trying to decide if I was going to call for her panties or her bra. I'd never seen what was under either and I got a woody just thinking about it.

She drew two cards and shuffled them without looking, then held them close to her face and squeezed out the hand nice and slow with a whistle or a hmmm after each card was exposed.

"Straight," Grammy said. "Read 'em and weep." She turned her cards over one at a time, torturing me with the slowness and when she finished, I said, "Full," and threw them face up on the table all at once.

"What'll it be, big boy, the twins or Miss Puss?" she asked, acknowledging my superior full house.

Mom, leaning against the door jamb, cleared her throat.

Beat the Mirror

When I was young, I remember my mother saying, "Knock it off or I'll tell your father you've been at the mirror again."

I don't know why it upset them so much. I loved mirrors. I realized when I was three that if I stared into a mirror and then moved my head quickly I believed I could fake out the mirror and my image would stay there a little longer before going about its business. I believed there was another me there; not just a reflection. No one believed me. Once, they stopped our family Sunday dinner and made me go into the bathroom and prove it in the mirror over the sink. It didn't work that time and I was warned to stop fibbing or else.

Or else usually meant my father smacking me somewhere between my neck and knees, depending on how much I squirmed.

When Mitzi was eight I showed her, but first made her pinky swear to keep it to herself. She said she didn't see it but I saw a quick flash of us holding hands. And all these years since, I haven't shown it to anyone, not even Mitzi again, not even on our wedding night.

I've watched little kids try to beat the mirror and have wanted to explain how to do it but it's like trying to teach someone to wiggle their ears—you're either a wiggler or you're not.

Mitzi would have been eighty-two today. I miss her but I keep busy puttering and keeping the lawn and her flowerbeds looking pretty and she would have liked that. The kids want me to move in with them but I'd rather be alone in our house—Mitzi's and mine.

I got into my pajamas and washed up and brushed my teeth and turned away from the mirror then, for some reason, quickly looked back which I haven't done since I can't remember when. I saw nothing this time, but tonight I was okay with that.

Daddy's Way

I got down on my knees and begged for leniency. The power of my father's belt thundered down time after time until my back was raw and his arm spent.

He said he believed in tough love. That's bully talk for picking on the weaker and less fortunate. He's right about one thing, though. I won't forget to take out the garbage again.

Helen and Ellen

Oh no! This is all I need now—Walker the Stalker coming towards me on the moving sidewalk and I can't get off and he's going to see me and after all these years it'll start again just like in high school.

If I wasn't pulling my suitcase I'd turn and run upstream like a salmon to get away. This airport's so crowded I know I could lose him. Maybe if I keep my head down and turned he won't notice me.

I already feel like shit after Ellen's funeral and even though we were twins, we weren't close. She liked losers and became one herself. Hell—she even liked this creep, Tommy Walker, who wouldn't give her a tumble because he wanted me.

Shit—I shouldn't have peeked. He's staring at me. It's been twenty years or more but, oh shit, now he's smiling and lifting his roll-on. He's not dumb enough to jump from his side to mine, is he? Of course he is. He's waiting for me to notice him and smile back. All I want to do is get to the luggage carousel and pick up the box with Ellen's ashes and get away from here.

He's about to talk but I beat him to it. I put my hand on his and force a smile: "Ellen," I say and he puts down his suitcase as his smile fades and I continue towards Ellen knowing I'll tell her the story at the cemetery tomorrow.

Kiss Kiss

Grandma will be wearing a mask when we visit so don't you kids be alarmed.

How will we know it's Grandma under the mask?

It's just a mask that covers her mouth so she doesn't breath in germs.

Grandma's scary. Can we cover our eyes with a mask so we're not afraid?

Is she going to take off her mask when she gives us her squishy wet hello and goodbye kisses?

No kissing this time. Germs. Grandma's now afraid of germs.

What about the money? Will she still give us money if she doesn't kiss us?

Maybe she'll say 'kiss kiss' and give you a check. She doesn't touch money anymore since she read that money's covered with germs from many people.

Can we wear masks too? We can say 'kiss kiss' and hand her pictures we've drawn.

Is she going to cook that stew again she always cooks?

No. We'll stop at a restaurant before we go to her house and get lunch. We'll bring her lunch from there also.

You can show her your pictures but if she's not wearing doctor's gloves she won't touch them. Remember, say hello and then go out in the yard and play and I'll come get you when it's time to leave.

Why don't we stay home and you tell Grandma we're waiting in the car so we don't bring in germs?

If she doesn't see you she probably won't give you any money and you know we're broke and need money.

Can't you just tell that to Grandma?

No. Grandma likes to play this game so we have to go along with her.

Do you still want me to go into her bedroom and look for jewelry?

Yes. Remember, only one piece and try to remember that it should have diamonds.

What about me? What should I look for?

Look for cash in the usual places. Under the mattress and in her underwear drawer. Poke around the room and if you find any, take it all so she'll think she forgot where she put it.

Is Grandma going to die?

We're all going to die.

Should I still take her pills and put aspirin in the pill bottles?

Just in one pill bottle.

Sis

Mom and Sis fought ever since the day Sis put Mom through eighteen hours of labor. Mom didn't care for her much after that, which is not to say she didn't provide the basics but basics with no extras are pretty damn worthless.

We other three kids did our best to run interference for Sis, which became her birth certificate name since Mom had no desire to moniker her up with a flower or saint name. Unlike us boys, she thought Sis was bound to grow up looking hard and she wasn't about to give her a soft name.

Sis looked like Mom and Mom hated hearing it. They had the same hitch in their voice and their mannerisms were alike which drove Mom crazy and she kept her head turned away when speaking to her.

The day Sis started high school Mom let her know that she was expected to get a job like us guys but, unlike us, was expected to move out after graduation.

Sis turned out to be the best student of all and got a scholarship to State. Mom's only comment was they must be making classes easier.

After graduation, which all of us but Mom went to, even though we begged her to join us, we guys threw a party for Sis at our house and had buckets of Kentucky Chicken, a keg, and mounds of donut holes which friends and family used to make a toast and say a few words of praise about Sis. Then Mom spoke.

"I bet you can't wait to get out of this hell-hole and be with your uppity friends," Mom said.

"They're not uppity, they're smart," Sis said

"Your graduation present's in your bedroom," Mom said. "You should go up and start using it."

Sis came down a while later, dragging a big suitcase and asked us two brothers to bring down the other two suitcases and the box sitting on top of them.

Sis pulled a framed picture out of the box. "This is your high school graduation picture, Mom."

Mom wouldn't turn her head to look at the picture so Sis walked around the living room and kitchen holding the picture next to her face and listened as the guests all talked about their similarity. Mom's face bunched red and angry. Then Sis propped her Mom's picture and her own up on the mantle and walked over and took a drumstick.

Superpowers

My wife says she can hear the neighbors and she heard them again last night having make-up sex. I tell her that she has superpowers and I'm impressed because I obviously don't have them since I don't hear our neighbors. She teases me and says I'm plain envious she has an ability that I don't and I tell her I can't argue with that statement and she says good thing and I say having superpowers *is* a good thing. She goes back to her crossword puzzle and without looking at me says *Sorry, did you say something to me*? I answer telepathically so I can have my own superpower.

Watch Me

Watch me, Mom, watch. Dad, Dad watch me. C'mon watch. You never watch me anymore since the new baby.

I'm reading the paper. Let me be—I'll watch you later.

The paper's not going anywhere, Dad. Watch me.

C'mon, Mom. Watch.

I'm doing the crossword puzzle—let me be.

Watch! Will someone watch me pleeease?

Where the hell did he get a gun?

Weren't you watching him? I was reading the paper.

I was doing the crossword puzzle. Weren't you supposed to keep that gun locked up? My baby, oh, my baby.

Call an ambulance!

Why didn't he say something?

Winter Walks

Hand, she says. We walk, our long winter coats touching. Before we reach the corner, her hand searches for mine. Gloveless, it's in my pocket trying to keep warm. Don't always make me ask for your hand, she says, through clenched teeth. As always, I apologize and reach up for her hand.

Hand, I say, and she ignores me, instead stands holding her four-pronged cane, her black shoes resting on the curb. Hand, I say again, and she ignores me still, showing her stubbornness, waiting for me to lift her gloved hand from her side and hold it while crossing the street. Once we're across, Mom rubs her hand on my sleeve and squeezes my arm, and then sets off heading into the wind, her coat pressed against her, anxious to end our weekly lunch and get to her apartment for her daily bridge game.

Wallflower Solution

My wife said, "If you're going to just stand in a corner alone with a drink in your hand all night and not speak to anyone there's no sense in our going to this party. You can only spend so much time looking at their photos and paintings and pouring over their book cases like you're a CIA agent. You've got to talk to people because they know you're avoiding them and they think you're rude and you think you're better than everyone else."

"You know that's not how I think," I told Elaine. "I'm no good at small talk and somehow when I get in these situations I feel inferior and awkward. I do talk to people when they come over and say hello."

"Well, that's the point. You need to make the effort. Last time we went to the Kleins' you studied their books and then read for most of the night. That was rude and if you keep being rude and stand-offish we are not going to get invited to any more parties and then what will we do?"

"Well, Mirsky, you really did it this time. I'm afraid to show my face after the performance you put on tonight," Elaine said after our silent car ride home and when we finally got into bed.

"I don't know what you're unhappy about. I spoke to everyone at the party like you wanted me to. I didn't look at the artwork or books and stayed away from all of the corners. In fact, I stationed myself in the center of the living room for a good part of the evening."

"We were at the home of an artist and a rare book collector," Elaine said. "You ignored both the art and the books and spent your time making the smallest of small talk. You're an embarrassment."

"The next party we go to why don't you fill me in on the things I should and shouldn't look at and the topics I ought to discuss and the ones I should avoid," I asked. "I want to do this party thing right and please you."

"Telling a woman her dress shows off her cleavage perfectly is not a way to start a conversation," Elaine said. "I'll make you up a crib sheet of conversation openers and current events and even compliments for you to keep with you and then you can go into the bathroom every once and a while to refresh your memory."

"It's better than talking about the weather which I refuse to do."

"There are other things besides weather and cleavage, you know."

"Actually I didn't know. I will use your crib sheet the next time we go to one of these cocktail parties."

"I don't know how you did it, Mirsky, but you were wonderful at the Levines' tonight. I saw you mixing with groups and singles and smiling all night. What were you talking about that got you out of your shell?"

"It was easier than I thought it would be," I said.

Elaine hugged me and told me how proud of me she was. "What do you think made the difference?" she asked.

"The crib sheet," I said.

"Did you memorize it? Wow, who would have thought that writing a few notes down would be the catalyst in changing a life-long behavior pattern."

The next morning at breakfast Elaine answered the phone and call after call came in so she never had a chance to eat her eggs before they turned cold. I ate and read the paper feeling good and looked up at Elaine and smiled as I heard her talk to each caller about the party. Elaine wasn't smiling back; in fact, she had "her face" look going.

Finally, during a lull in the calls, Elaine told me that all the calls were about me and how personable and funny I was.

"That's nice," I said.

"For you maybe, but not so nice for me," Elaine said. "You showed everyone the crib sheet and asked them to pick a topic," she said. "So all of the laughter I saw going on with you was about me—is that it?"

"They thought you were a riot," I said. "And they're looking forward to the next get-together to see my new set of instructions."

TSA: Here to Serve, Here to Help

Mendel stood waiting to board the plane.

He took off his shoes, emptied his pockets, turned on his computer and stepped into the x-ray machine with his hands up. No alarms went off but he was still escorted to the TSA headquarters where they questioned him for three hours and water boarded him twice.

Then he was taken into another room, allowed to shower, shave, and given a set of expensive clothes and told to sit on the couch facing a wall. It was painted olive drab, a color he hadn't thought about since his military days, and that made it easy to sit immobile at attention. After 22 minutes the wall parted, opening curtain-like, and he was looking out at a studio audience who gave him a robust round of applause.

He remained seated while the TSA water boarders brought his luggage in. Behind the audience was a full wall of windows and Mendel saw the airport and a large commercial jet sitting on the tarmac. Motioning for Mendel to stand, the TSA agents escorted him up a long aisle through the crowd. Some people waved handkerchiefs while others held "Free Mendel" signs. People on the aisle put out their hands for high fives and fist bumps until Mendel reached the ticket agent's counter and secure door where the attendants gave him his boarding pass.

The crew waited at the door, checked his ticket, and a flight attendant took him by the arm and led him through first and business classes to coach and then to a middle seat in the rear across from the bathroom between a five-year-old and a large man overflowing his seat. As the plane began to taxi, the flight attendant showed everyone how their seat belt worked.

The Woman with the Juicy Fruit Breath

Mirsky, out for a drive to get away from the house and think, was in downtown Branford when he looked over and saw a woman dressed in a white suit; flared white pants, matching jacket and a button down white silk-like shirt with long pointy collars. The only touch of color was a red boutonnière which did not match her red hair. Her arms were filled with papers and Mirsky wondered why she didn't have them in a briefcase or mailbag of some sort.

He thought back to a woman he once saw in New York wearing a similar outfit but not as attractive and not as well put together. He looked from the woman to the road ahead and jammed on his brakes. He heard the car behind him do the same. She was kneeling down gathering the papers that had spilled onto the street as she began to cross, trying to keep them from blowing further away. He wondered if he should get out and help her when the car behind him began blowing its horn belligerently. Looking in his rear view mirror he saw an angry twisted face and a man making closed fist gestures at him. He thought of putting his car in park and going over to the car and telling him that there was a woman picking up papers in front of him and he couldn't move without running her over.

Turning back from the mirror the woman was standing back on the sidewalk as before, after gathering her papers. Mirsky waved to the man behind him and drove off circling the block. He made two right turns and found a parking space near the corner and pulled over. The woman in white was no longer on the sidewalk and Mirsky, disappointed as could be, figured that her ride came along and picked her up or she crossed the street and went into one of the stores or offices and then he noticed the store sign—Luggage. No one's name indicating who owned the store and the sign wasn't even attractive but pitted and paint worn.

Strange, he thought. All the years I've been on this street I never noticed that store. It was nestled between Mrs. Murphy Toys for Tweens and Risko Appliances. He crossed over to the esplanade and then walked to the store. It was a small storefront with a glass door that needed cleaning and a picture window that was almost beyond cleaning with samples of suitcases and briefcases haphazardly thrown in.

The bell tinkled as he opened the door and an older pumpkin of a woman with wire rim glasses and disheveled stringy grey-black hair told him to look around she'd be with him in a few minutes. The store was jam-packed with merchandise, pack-rat style, showing both the newest designs and very old, some of which were in vogue again.

He heard talking and turned towards the sound as the woman in white walked up to him. "Thanks for stopping your car so I could pick up my papers," she said. "I wanted to throw my arms out wide in apology but that would've just tossed more papers around."

"I actually wanted to get out and help you," Mirsky said, "but the driver behind me was blasting his horn and shaking his fist."

"I'm sorry. It really is true that no good deed goes unpunished."

"It's not the worst road rage I've seen. While you were standing on the sidewalk holding all those papers I was thinking you should have a mailbag or briefcase of some kind and then the next thing I knew you were in the road in front of me picking up your papers."

"In that case, take a look at a couple of bags I've picked out and tell me which you think would suit me." Her Wrigley's Juicy Fruit breath came floating his way and Mirsky had the urge to taste the flavor on her lips.

She was striking, her red hair cascading over her white clad shoulders made him think back to an encounter many years earlier when he was a young man. She turned and went back deeper into the store where she'd come from and he walked over to a shelf and took down a cordovan bag with white rivet edges to bring to her.

"Now what is it I can help you with?" the rumpled proprietress asked.

Looking around, Mirsky didn't see the woman with the Juicy Fruit breath. "I was bringing this back to show the woman in white," he said.

"There's no one here but you, are you auditioning for a job?" she asked.

Mirsky shook his head and wanted to call Elaine to come and get him. She was understanding and had done so before when he left the house without telling her. She wouldn't ask him any questions except if he'd like a new briefcase or piece of luggage.

Mirsky wanted to be home sitting in his chair thinking scenarios, feeling warm and safe but at the sound of the saleswoman's voice he snapped alert and asked if he could take a phone picture of the cordovan bag to show his wife. "She doesn't like surprises but she does like nice presents," Mirsky said and then left the store. He made a quick right out the door never looking left where the woman in white was standing, a cordovan bag with white rivets dangling from her shoulder.

Deal or no Deal

I walked over to my vinyl collection and put on Elvis' 'Love Me Tender', the song that still, at age fifty-five, gave me chills and a twitch in my shorts. Our martinis, Sari's gin and my vodka, sat on the coffee table waiting. I dimmed the lights, reached in my pocket, took out a small velvet bag, walked over and picked up my martini. Sari took hers. We clinked glasses and she said "My turn" and made a toast. "May your grooves on this record disappear as it's playing."

Undeterred by her humor, knowing how I felt about this song, we clinked glasses, sipped and smiled at each other. I'm not a down on one knee kind of guy so I sat on the loveseat and handed her the little velvet bag. She smiled at me and then smelled it and shook it by her ear as if the sound would give its contents away and finally she untied the loose cabled string.

"Hurry up," I blurted, "the fucking song's almost over."

Sari shook the diamond ring into her hand as Elvis sang "... never let me go."

"Talk to me," Sari said handing me the ring.

"I love you. Marry me. Whatdoyasay? Let's get married."

I took Sari's left hand and slipped the ring on. It was a one and a half carat round sparkler that looked at home on her fifty-two-year-old liver-spotted hand.

"Only if you let me break that record."

"I will after we get home from our honeymoon and dance to it our first night back," I said.

"But it dries out my insides. Can't you change to Johnny Mathis singing 'Chances Are'? Now that's a song that gets me wet. I've hurt your feelings, but Herby used to put that on every time he wanted some action. Do you want me thinking about Herby when we do it?"

"I love you enough to do it," I said, "but you have to do something for me."

"Sure, anything, tell me."

"No more mac 'n cheese."

"Huh?"

"No more in the house or out. I hate the look, the smell and did I mention the look of that orange cheese? The glop sound it makes when spooned onto a plate. The stain it leaves on your lips and the god awful mac 'n cheese breath. Need I go on?"

"But mac 'n cheese is my guilty pleasure, my comfort food. You know that."

"I do, but I feel very strongly about this."

"Very strongly?"

"Yes. Very," I said.

Sari looked at her hand, turned it back and forth letting the dim light sparkle off the diamond and then reached for her glass and finished her drink.

"Mix me another," she said.

Trade

At lunch everyone in our IT section leaves our cubicles and goes to the lunch room and the eight of us sit at the same back corner table and chat and eat. Today five of us had brown bags and the other three had lunch boxes: Sponge Bob, Spidey and a pond scene from a Monet painting. Before opening our lunch someone asked, "Trade?" (someone always asks) and two brown bags were exchanged. This day there were three trades, two bags and a lunch box and there were lots of good-natured nasty food comments. After lunch, we went back to our cubicles and I looked over at Marty, who finally opened his lunch bag, took out his sandwich and drink and laid his head in his arms and wept just as he had been doing every day since the lunch Trade began.

Uncle Harry's Last Magic Trick

During Uncle Harry's visits he dazzled me with magic. At six he held my nose, tapped my head, nickels tumbled out. At eight he pulled quarters from my ear. At eleven he reached up my skirt to pull a ten dollar bill out as Dad walked into the room.

Stalemate

I am in charge of traffic in New Haven. I control the traffic lights. From the computer on my desk I can make driving smooth or I can make it a nightmare. If I didn't have this power I would have to find power somewhere else.

I sit at my desk, across from the three six foot screens watching and coordinating lights to allow for firemen and policemen to speed through intersections as safely as possible.

My brother is an air traffic controller and he tells me that I don't know what power is. He says he can make people late for their connections by keeping them in the air or on the taxiway for real or imagined reasons. He told me that he once told a landing Delta jet to "go around" because there was a dog on the runway. He laughed when he told me that, so I told him how I once kept the lights on Church and Chapel and Church and Elm all green to create a traffic jam that lasted over an hour.

My brother and I have nothing in common except trying to one up the other in our "control" stories. My wife won't fly into Newark when he's on duty and his wife won't come into New Haven when I'm at work so we have to meet at a neutral site if we're going to get together. My brother knows that I know the other traffic lighters in the area so he won't set a get-together spot in advance.

He acts all spy-like and wants to call me while I'm on the turnpike heading in a given direction and tell me where to meet. I can't have him controlling me so I tell him I'll go to a city or resort and call him to meet us. He won't do it because then he's not in control. If there weren't family get-togethers like weddings, funerals and bar mitzvahs we'd never see each other.

The Blame Game

Every morning, when I leave my house for work, I have to run to my car as my neighbors shoot rock salt at me with shotguns.

Why me and not their wives, who took turns bringing warm casseroles and hot bodies when my wife left me?

Speaking of My Father

I said that I didn't know him and that he abandoned my mother and us three boys, ages five, four and one.

Obviously he's a man without character I told this stranger who had sought me out and was drinking CC with a beer chaser. I was drinking Bud long necks.

Do you think he's got any redeeming qualities?

Maybe in appearance but not at heart.

Do any of you brothers resemble him?

Who knows I said and we both turned and looked at the other and saw ourselves, one older, one younger. I swiveled and ordered a double CC.

Sand

Yesterday we kind of buried Uncle Bert. He was married to Mom's sister Pearl and thought he was God's gift to the women of this world. Unfortunately for him we found out he had been putting the moves on Mom and her sister Tess and sister-in-law Deb.

He was wearing Mom down, my sister Rita told me and our brothers Ricky and Todd. We called our cousins who had been experiencing the same feelings about their mothers and Uncle Bert.

Me and my brothers and our cousins waylaid Uncle Bert as he was getting into his car after leaving the Dew Drop Inn around ten-thirty last night. We held him down and duct taped his mouth, legs and wrapped the tape around his body, pinning his arms to his sides.

We dragged his heavy ass into the back of Matt T.'s pickup and went down the beach a couple blocks from our houses where we dug a trench and tossed him in, eyes staring up at us not in fear but in anger. For good measure we each threw a shovelful of sand on him.

We passed a joint, swearing each other to secrecy and went home for the night.

Just as the sun was coming up, Rick, Todd and I were awakened by the honking of horns. We looked out the window and saw Uncle Bert standing straight up still duct taped, taking small hops trying to cross the street to our house. I called our cousins who came rushing over, beating Uncle Bert across the street.

We knew he'd kill us once he got loose so we talked about burying him deeper but instead decided to call the cops and report a strange man all bound up.

They came, cut him loose from the duct tape and sat him on our porch, questioning him. He said he was caught from behind and had no idea who did it or why. After the police left, he didn't say a word to us about the incident.

Later that night when Aunt Pearl came to pick him up she told us they've been looking at houses in Florida and this was the push they needed to move out of the cold northeast.

I asked Uncle Bert if he thought they'd be living near a beach and he said, "You bet, so you boys will have to come down and visit. The sand is beautiful, you'll love it."

Dummy

Dad wasn't always a dummy but the day he quit working for my grandfather making custom eyelets for shoes and boots he turned into one for Consumer Car Tests. He tests cars going two or three miles an hour while strapped into his seat belt in different sitting locations. The car always plows into a six foot high steel beam turned vertical and buried deep in concrete. There's also a programmable dummy strapped in and it can be read like an airplane's black box.

At dinner tonight Dad sat at his place in the kitchen and held his head up with one hand and spooned soft food into his mouth with the other. His lip was split and his right eye swollen closed and ringed in purple.

"How many days do you have off from work?" Mom asked.

"Just two," he croaked. "No need for a hospital visit but I tried."

"Henry," Mom said. "Maybe it's time to swallow your pride and go back working for your father."

Dad spooned some blended meat and grunted an equivalent of "no".

Meanwhile, I-Lets, his father's company, with this name change implemented by my dad, along with major factory and marketing changes he suggested, went from a once failing company into the far-and-away number one eyelet company in the country. His father took credit for the changes and refused Dad a partnership or a substantial raise.

Dad got a call a year to the day after he left the company. "Don't be a dummy, Henry. Come back and we'll work something out."

"Tell me the terms first," Dad said.

"No, dummy, come back first and show me the respect and trust and then we'll talk."

Dad hung up on his father.

For a dummy he was making good money but was always too tired or sore to enjoy it and to top it off he couldn't qualify for health insurance. Mom told us all at dinner that she had gotten a job and was going to be a receptionist in a real estate office and would be studying to get her license and become a sales person. Mom's only experience was selling cosmetics at a five and dime and often said, "If I can get people to buy that stuff I can sell anything."

Dad could only grunt with his jaw wired shut. He was out on sick pay for two months after his seat belt in the Korean car he was testing broke and he went through the window and into one of the steel beams. Now he has to eat his food using a straw.

When Dad saw Mom's first couple of paychecks he offered to bring her into the business where she could make real money, but Mom was no dummy.

Destination Wedding

Sandy and Ben's sitter called in sick, so, against Sandy's better wishes, they left their ten-year-old son and his grandfather alone while they went to the wedding. Ben kept telling Sandy not to worry so she worried more and called home often until it became too late to call. Texts went unanswered.

Sandy's concerns made them both have a miserable time at the wedding so they drove home silently, in the middle of the night, instead of staying over as planned. She never forgave Ben or their son for letting her father wander away and never seeing him again.

Epilogue

A month shy of five years, Bill and Sally had a visit from the FBI who gave them the news that their daughters were fine, not abducted, and living in mid-state Connecticut with two men they left with voluntarily five years earlier. No reason given.

The following week a cab dropped Lori and Shelly off at their old home they hadn't seen since their disappearance. Without knocking, they walked into the unlocked house and not seeing or hearing anyone, went up to their old bedrooms. Nothing had changed. Dolls and stuffed animals still littered their beds and their clothes were in their walk-in closets.

They went down to the kitchen and picked through the refrigerator and checked out the cookie canister. Then they walked out to the back yard. Their parents, Bill and Sally, were sitting by the pool where the lawn sloped down in gentle rolls to Long Island Sound and their private beach.

"Hi," Lori said. "We're home."

Bill and Sally stood to greet the girls and Lori and Shelly walked down and they were hugged briefly and awkwardly. No kisses or words were exchanged and their father took his seat and motioned for them to sit.

For over four years the girls were thought of as being abducted and huge rewards were offered and every year on the anniversary of their going missing the local TV station did a segment on the family.

All this time, they were living in trailers on five acres of land and were long haul truck drivers, just as their men were. There was going to be a big to-do in the newspaper and the local TV station about their return home, the prominence of their father assured that.

They gave a couple of small interviews, let the photographers take some pictures but said very little except that they weren't abducted and were just ready for a change. They didn't give the names of their boyfriends or tell where they'd been living.

Lori and Shelly moved back into the house without discussing it with their parents, who they now called Bill and Sally, and stayed for a couple of months lounging by the pool, going to the Club with them, and even connecting with a few old friends.

They were solicitous of Bill and Sally, cleaned up after themselves, made some family dinners, but never spoke of anything in depth. Bill and Sally had become uncomfortable with this arrangement and one day, at cocktail hour, Bill asked his daughters what their plans were. "Are you planning to live here? What about work and do you plan to disappear again and leave us wondering?"

The girls said they'd hang around a bit but as to disappearing again, well, let's play that one loose.

I Have a Problem

I have a problem. Well I have more than one but this one is Yuge. I can't work in a mess and I can't not make a mess where I work. My office looks like the shredder truck should back in and take care of things but I called them and they won't drive to the second floor. My wife who has the neatness thing down opens my office door sticks her hand in and sprays something every once in a while. She told me that curing my problem was easy. "There are only three things you do with a piece of paper, a – file it, b – toss it or, c – hand it off to someone else." She won't let me hand papers off to her. Easy for her to say but I don't have that gene and I would like to talk to a doctor about it but most of them are slobs too. I did go to see a shrink a couple of years ago and I started out by telling him I fall asleep constantly, especially when I sit and that's the car, movies anywhere. I also planned to tell him about this mess problem but we parted company when he yelled at me for falling asleep while he was talking to me. I told him he ought to see someone about the attitude. My neighbor's at my door. I have a hunch he's the one calling me in a fake Indian accent trying to tell me that he got a signal that my Windows computer has a problem. Only this time he wanted to complain about my koi pond. How the hell can you complain about something as benign as a koi pond? It's relatively easy he said and I caught him slipping into that fake Indian accent and he knew I did and mumbled something about a barbecue and crept away as quickly as he came. I don't want to sound crazy but I think my papers are fucking and reproducing when I'm not in the office. I say nasty things to telemarketers who call me with this Microsoft shit or solar panels or my winning another free trip to the Bahamas. I ask them to hold on for a second because I'm just getting ready to take a picture of their wife and a goat for welovebestiality.com. Sometimes I tell the caller he's interrupting a prayer service or I have to call him back the undertaker just drove up. It seems now that I don't really have a problem—people who come in contact with me do and I plan to keep it that way.

Introducing Bennie
the Magnificent

Nine-year-old Bennie dreamed of being a magician. He booked a birthday party for a five-year-old. He made rubber balls double in number then disappear. He did card tricks and the colored scarf trick. He cut a rope in half, tied it in a knot and abbra kadabra slid the knot up and down and made it whole again. Bennie pulled a white rabbit from a hat then put it in the special box he made—ears and feet sticking out. He began to saw. "Oh, crap!" Bennie said.

I've Had My Fill

It started out with the squirrels. They were eating me out of house and birdfeeder. Then it was the chipmunks, darting back and forth, stealing from my garden, frolicking around and not giving two shits for anyone or anything. The raccoons, what the hell can I say about these fat little bastards who can figure out how to open my "coon-proof" garbage can and eat what they want and toss everything else on the ground, creating a constant mess for me to clean up.

They're all mostly gone, except for the birds, but they're safe for now. I'm going vegan.

Kaboom!

Because I read a passage that spoke of them, I hear the sound of church bells. The librarian shoots me a look. I must've scraped my chair or something. Gunshots—I need an aspirin. Maybe the librarian has one but she glares at me again. This morning I drove in to a school bus while texting and got concussed. These noises never happened before unless I was playing "Mimic" with my family, but those were mostly voices and I turned out to be the best mimic.

I close my book. I begin to write and in the opening scene the Pope walks out onto his greeting balcony and everyone in the courtyard looks up, applauding and cheering. I wish I had a volume switch in my head. The noise makes me tug my right ear and it gets louder. I try my left and it softens. What the hell! What a godsend. I think about getting on my motor-cycle and heading to the hills of Italy but first I rev it up. Boy is it loud in my head. I tug my left ear and smile.

"This is a library and not a sound effects studio," the librarian says, towering above me, arms folded, face con-torted, bun shaking.

"What seems to be the problem?" I ask her.

"The problem is you're sitting in a library surrounded by quiet sounds and you're making noises—church bells, motorcycle, applause, and who knows what else. I'm going to have to ask you to leave if you do it again. You're disturbing our other patrons."

How can she hear what's going on in my head? Maybe she should pull her left ear lobe to turn down the volume.

She scowls.

I walk over to a college-age man a few tables away and ask him. I explain about the concussion and the sounds and I give him ear instructions and go back to my seat. I read the church bell paragraph again and he nods his head. I motion an ear pull and he yanks his left lobe and shakes his head. And then, I try again, hoping for . . . Again, he pulls his left lobe and shakes his head.

I'm fucked.

The librarian sits down and the splat of a whoopee cushion goes off. I chuckle but she's out of her chair and heading my way so I grab my bag and leave.

I walk out to the sound of a bicycle with a playing card hitting the spokes.

Dear Editor

Dear Editor,

Please cancel our subscription. I can no longer have your newspaper lying around where my children can read the "Letters to the Editor" advocating same sex marriage, separation of church and state, atheist rights, teaching of sex education in school, locations where free condoms are dispensed, transgender studies (whatever they are), school book lists with teen pregnancies, gay themes, sex talk of any kind and cuss words, talking about the good Planned Parenthood does (without mentioning the harm), help for abused women, pregnant girls, rogue cops, gun laws, medical marijuana, pro choice, shorter jail sentencing, Black Lives Matter, and pro-immigration.

After all, this is America. Read your Constitution and Bill of Rights or better yet, print them in your Anti-God, anti-family, and anti-American newspaper.

Very truly yours,

Marcus and Mary Ellen Higganum
Proprietors of Lock and Load Firearms and The Booze Barn

PS: long time subscribers and advertisers.
PPS: We are also considering pulling our advertising.

Too Many Uncles

I'm Momma just before she's ready to go out. Her date will be here any minute, honk his horn and she'll be off—blowing us kisses and telling us to be good and not to stay up too late. Watch the baby, she'll say and then we won't see her for at least a day.

I'm Momma and just woke up and it's noon. I'll take a little of my medicine from the big bottle and add some tomato juice and I'll feel better. Here—take the baby, I can't stand his fidgeting, Go! Take him away before he starts crying.

I was dancing last night with my date and then he got tired and sat down to drink and I kept dancing and I didn't have to sit down to drink—I can drink standing up and dancing and he didn't like that and called me names and drove off without me.

Keep baby quiet. The nice man who gave me a ride home is still sleeping. He saw me walk by the door and must have thought I was Momma cause he said, C'mere sugar. I kept walking and then I snuck a look back in the room and he was sleeping. He can snore up a storm.

I want you to go put Baby down next to Momma on the couch. She's taking her medicine and smoking and she can watch for a while and you and me will go out shopping. I have her purse and car keys. Grab me a couple of her cigarettes so I'll look older as we drive. No she won't get mad.

We'll tell her that she sent us shopping and told us to take her purse and her car keys. Do we say anything about the money we took from that man's pants? I didn't think so. We can buy us some nice makeup and bring home another baby—a girl this time. Momma's not gonna be happy.

We'll bring her one of those big bottles of her medicine and she'll be fine. Let's drive by the school and honk the car horn and then go buy a reefer and share it. Think Momma's going out tonight?

Depends. When we get home and she has us call him Uncle than he'll be around for a while and Momma will only go out on the weekend. Yeah, I'm tired of the Uncles, too, cause they think I'm Momma's sister.

Do you think we have any real Uncles?

Drivers' Rules

If I turn right I'll have to turn right two more times.

If I don't turn right I'll have to make a u-turn and take my chances.

A left turn isn't an option on a Street—only a Road.

A Lane is the same as a "Get Out of Jail Free" card—no rules.

A Boulevard is the toughest; a right turn from the left lane or a left turn from the right lane—no signaling allowed—just gun and go.

I'm afraid not to follow these rules but I wish I knew who was leaving them on my windshield.

I Had No Choice.
I Had to Let
My Cleaning Lady Go

She said she was a radiologist in Russia but the US wouldn't accept her credentials so she did what she had to do to take care of her elderly mother and young daughter. She said her husband and father were not allowed to leave because they worked in the defense industry,

So, Sasha and her mother both got divorces and came to the USA with the little one, hoping for a good life and maybe a couple of rich husbands, but nothing yet on that front.

Sasha came every Tuesday and Friday. She cleaned, cooked, washed and ironed the clothes and taught my seventeen-year-old son the pleasures of sex. I knew about the cooking and ironing and stuff but not about the sex.

She tried to put the moves on me and I can't say I wasn't tempted but I didn't touch her even though she was gorgeous and stacked. She would tell me knock-knock jokes and get the punch lines reversed. That alone made me want her. Her stuffed cabbage and beef stew were award winners and I never got up the nerve to talk with her about underwear. Hers not mine.

I wore. She didn't. "In Russia women in my village, we all commando," she told me once when she saw my eyes stray. I was reading the paper and she was ironing, both of us in the kitchen, and I didn't have the air conditioner on and every ten minutes or so Sasha would unbutton another button on her blouse until it was totally open and her breasts swayed with her arm as she ironed. She never looked at me but she would take the shirt by the shoulders and snap it before turning it over and with every snap, her blouse separated and she stood there exposed and nonchalant.

I was so close to giving in you have no idea. "Mister, a cold glass water, maybe?" She'd take one for herself, lean against the kitchen counter, put her foot on a chair, and there she was—full commando. And always with a look of innocence as if it was a perfectly normal way to walk around your boss' house.

I asked my son, Peter, what he'd like for his eighteenth birthday and he told me he's been giving it a lot of thought and knew that I was fair and generous and I said, "Go ahead, hit me with it."

"I want to marry Sasha," he said. "She's only eight years older than me and I love her."

"How do you know you love her?" I asked, and it turned out that Sasha, although I believe I was her first choice, was willing to settle for Peter, who she found out had nothing like his father's will power.

"Sasha, is it true you've been sleeping with Peter?" I asked.

"Not once," she said. "Who told you that lie?"

"Peter did," I said.

"Peter and I make sex but never sleep," she said.

I explained to her the law on sex with minors. Well, actually I had two friends, my attorney and a uniformed police captain, come to the house and explain it so there would be no misunderstanding.

After my lawyer and the Police Captain left I asked Sasha to follow me upstairs and I walked into my bedroom for a proper goodbye. She followed me and buttoned her blouse as she stood defiantly in the doorway, looking down at me on my bed and then lifted her skirt. "No commando," she showed me and said, "Sasha no whore for you."

She left me no choice. I had to let her go.

A Pinball Day
in the Projects

Ray Hayman was not only tough but crazy. Out of school as much as in—fighting, stealing lunch money and bagged lunches too. He was lean but muscular and only 5'6" and even the football players kept their distance.

He lived a half dozen buildings over in the projects. His apartment was on my paper route and every so often when I rang the bell for the weekly payment his mother would tell me to wait and Ray would come to the door. "Hi Ray," I'd say and he'd say, "No jingle this week," take the paper, then shut the door and I'd nod and chalk it up to a business expense.

Once, he was inside the corner store playing pinball while a half dozen of us were milling around outside waiting for him to leave so we could play. I was the smallest and the chunkiest. The door opened and the other guys backed away and I said my usual, "Hi Ray," and he said, "Give me a quarter." All I had was a quarter and that was five games so I shook my head. "Sorry, Ray. Can't do," I said.

"I'm gonna kick your ass," he said, lunging head down to butt me in my soft belly, but fear took over and I grabbed the collar of his jacket and pulled it over his head and pushed it down and kneed him in the face twice and then, while his zipped-up jacket was still over his head I punched him in the head with rights and lefts until my hands hurt and when he pulled his jacket back, tears were streaming down his face and I knew I was going to get my ass kicked then but he said, "I'm going to tell my mother," and ran off.

Understand, now. I've had fights before and lost almost every one but this was different. My friends treated me like a hero and even paid for my first pinball game. Twenty minutes later, housecoat and apron flying, Mrs. Hayman stormed into the store and pointed at me.

"You Porky Pig little sombitch, you had no call to hurt my Raymond. When his brother gets out of prison in two weeks I'm sending him over to slice you up."

I tried to convince my mother we had to move and move quickly. She told me I shouldn't be fighting and if we could move we wouldn't be living in the projects.

Ray's brother Roy Albert Hayman was finally released from prison and his picture was on the *Bridgeport Post's* front page. He walked to a gas station after the bus dropped him off in some small town and he swiped car keys from a guy who was filling up and then went into the station and knifed the owner and cleaned out the register. He found a gun behind the counter and when the police showed up after getting a call from the driver who had his keys swiped and was hiding in the phone booth he blasted away at them trying to get to his getaway car. The gun jammed and he dropped it and put up his hands surrendering. He was tackled and beaten bloody and senseless and never made it home to slice me up and I don't expect he will so I stopped delivering papers to Ray's house and I never said, "Hi Ray," again.

Swinging

Why are you sitting watching TV and making a noose?

Just something to keep my hands busy.

Why don't you try crocheting?

Why don't you leave me alone?

We've been married eight years and you just started talking to me like that.

Like what?

Like you're doing and it's not nice.

Actually I'm hoping you'll like one of the nooses and take it down to the basement where I have a stool set up under a pipe.

Ben's eyes are like slits, his neck red and his teeth clenched.

Why won't you tell me why you're so mad at me?

Fuck off.

You know I don't like it when you use that language. Eve sniffs back a sob.

Fuck off. Fuck off. Fuck off. That language?

Maybe you should hang yourself with that noose.

You'd like that, wouldn't you?

Eve's eyes tear up, her hands shake and she nods her head.

Say it, damn it. Say it. He begins a new noose. He thinks to himself, *I begin a noose.*

You can at least have the decency to tell me why you're so angry at me. What did I do?

You know what you did. Everyone knows what you did but I was the last to find out.

Are you talking about me and Ernie?

What about you and Ernie?

Nothing. I was trying to figure you out.

Was it Alvey? Are you upset about me and Alvey?

Shouldn't I be?

No. It didn't mean anything. We were both drunk and he kissed me. That was it.

Ben slides the noose up and down the rope. Slip this over your head so I can check the fit.

I'll do no such thing. Well, was it Alvey? Jim—you've always been jealous of Jim. Right? It was Jim. Kimberly—right? We were cold and sharing a blanket. My cousin Tim—we're kissing cousins, always have been.

Ben shakes his head. You know, he says. You know.

You're right. I do know but I refuse to talk about it.

Tell me why. C'mon tell me why.

You know why. Who are you kidding?

I want to hear you say it. Nothing will be right between us until you do.

Where are you going?

I'll be in the basement.

Jimbo

James hated being called Jimbo but it became his nickname because his father always called him that and continued to when he realized that his son, who he was at constant loggerheads with, hated it. His mother called him James.

He thought when he joined the army things would change but he must've looked like a Jimbo because immediately in basic training his Drill Instructor began calling him Jimbo and it stuck through his years in the Middle East. He had made the mistake of telling his DI to call him James and not Jimbo. DIs, even ones a foot shorter than one of their soldiers, don't take to being corrected, especially in public and kicked his ass in front of the whole squadron after ordering Jimbo to throw the first punch. He threw a wicked left hook that could've shattered the DI's nose had he not been so quick as to lean back and then throw two shots rapid fire in Jimbo's gut and finish him off with a right cross to the eye that stayed black for a couple of weeks. He then gave the other soldiers orders to call him Jimbo or else.

He looked forward to his mother's frequent letters that always began "Dear James . . ."

When he returned home he moved into the house he grew up in at the end of a cul de sac. His father disappeared when he was a senior in high school and his mother died during his third tour. He was hopeful he'd be James to everyone but then he got a job in the IT department of a large company and ran into people from high school who jumped right back on the Jimbo train.

Afterwards, when the neighbors spoke to the press they had only good things to say about him but all said he was quiet and kept to himself and didn't seem to be violent in any way at all.

"He was a loner, but neither friendly nor unfriendly. He'd never be the first to say hello but he'd always respond with a nod or a hello back. He never asked us neighbors for help or us him."

"He kept his small lawn mowed and let the trees and bushes grow to the point of hiding parts of the house. He did keep his windows covered up 24/7."

"We all thought he worked in computers somewhere."

"No, I never had an extensive conversation with Jimbo. I don't think any of us on the street did. I just got back from vacation, why do you ask?"

"James, yes we called him James because that was his name. The families who lived here when he was growing up were the Jimbo people."

"He did seem to have more UPS deliveries than an average person."

"Nothing strange at all. He was one of those people who kept to himself."

"We had a block party every year and always invited him but he never came—never responded and never complained about the noise."

"No, he hadn't seemed any different lately."

"A weapon? No. I never saw him carry a weapon but you have to remember he drove in and out of his garage so no one saw much of him."

"Come to think of it you may be right—only the neighbors who called him Jimbo."

"No, I didn't hear any shots. No screams either and our windows were open."

"He got out of his car at the bus stop and was selective. That's what I heard."

"Only the people at work who called him Jimbo? Doesn't that beat all? He probably should've said something to them."

"They're going to dig up his yard looking for his father? You think you know someone and then something like this happens."

Cool Water

I'm spinning in my screened porch. Spinning faster than the overhead fan so I increase its speed and begin spinning again like I did as a five-year-old until I tried to stop and all wobbly legged, fell over laughing. I'm trying to avoid the wicker furniture and just before I go down for the count I see a man leaning against a cedar tree in my yard, watching me. As I fall I wonder if he would be watching if I were dressed in more than my bra and panties.

I've moved too close to the house and there's a chance she'll spot me but it's a chance I have to take. I've seen her in her pajamas and bathing suit but now, in her bra and panties, she's so gorgeous and her breasts are jiggling—they're jiggling a come on to me because by now she knows I'm watching.

I'm dizzy as fuck. Ha ha ha. That's such a silly thing to say but I can't get up and put on my shirt and walk down to the stream and undress again down to my spinning outfit and walk in the cool stream. I almost forgot I'm being watched by a man at the edge of my yard where the cedar grove is; maybe he wants to spin too. I'll just hold onto the wicker chair and get up but it spins around and I'm down again laughing like I was laughing when I was spinning. But wait, the table doesn't spin so I'll hold onto that and get up. Maybe I'll wave to the man in the woods.

She's waving to where I was standing before she fell. I knew I shouldn't have moved but I have a better view from here. She is so beautiful. She has got to be out of college because I haven't seen her since high school. Her bra has three snaps and is barely doing its job. My gosh! My gosh! I wonder if she'd like to walk down to the stream with me. We could take our shoes and socks off and roll up our pants and walk in the cool water. I could hold her hand at times so she wouldn't slip. She's not wearing shoes and socks. Maybe I'll invite her to walk to the stream and suggest she put on shoes and socks. I hope she stays dressed the way she is.

Here comes a car and behind it is my father's pickup. They are going to take me back and make her get dressed and all I want to do is walk in the stream with her. Well I won't move and they can't make me. My father looks so pissed and the other man is going into the house. He must be her father. Ooo trouble. Ooo trouble. But she's dressed and comes out on the front porch and says hello to my father and waves to me. Her father's behind her yelling something but she isn't paying attention. She looks my way and says hi, and I nod and smile and she comes down from the porch and takes my sweaty hand.

"Let's go walk in the stream," she says, still not wearing shoes or socks.

I Didn't Have a Ready Answer

We set out at 3am for New York. My GPS told me to take the Turnpike. My wife's iPhone told her to take the Interstate. My gut told me it's not going to matter so I took the Turnpike to the Parkway and a mile down the unlit Parkway we were blocked by stopped cars. After 15 minutes I got out and walked up to the front car to see what the holdup was and there was a line of pickups blocking the road and in front of each pickup was a man in CAMO carrying an automatic rifle. I walked up to the nearest man. "Hi," I said, "What seems to be the holdup?" He swerved and hit me in the side of my face with the rifle stock knocking me down. "What are you doing to make America Great Again?" he asked.

Dental Floss Debate: Good vs. Not So Good

Murph picked weeds for four of his neighbors from the age of five until he was eight. On his eighth birthday he passed out flyers, offering to shop, babysit or cleanup before or after parties or barbecues. When he was twelve he was allowed to have a paper route and built it up from fifty customers to almost a hundred. Along with that he mowed lawns and did odd jobs for some of his customers. Soon his mother gave up taking in laundry.

Murph was always in great demand. Mrs. Lacy tossed him a juicy tangerine after he handed her the paper and later on, while sitting on Mrs. Stewart's steps trying to get the silk from the tangerine out from between his teeth, Mrs. Stewart brought him a packet of dental floss and taught him how to use it. He carried the dental floss everywhere —and kept the new in one pocket and the used in the other.

Murph concentrated on making a dental floss ball and when it got to be four feet he hoisted it out of his basement with a fulcrum and put it on his childhood Radio Flyer red wagon and covered it with a SpongeBob sheet.

After that, he went around town charging a nickel to look at it and a dime to look and touch. He'd take your picture with it for a dollar and pretty soon, after the local papers featured him in an article, he was able to quit his other jobs and become a major contributor to the family's income, allowing his father to leave his second job.

All the while Murph continued adding to his now five-foot ball of floss. It grew to five and a half feet and became too heavy for him to roll into the basement so he went through the kitchen door, down the basement steps and over to the hatchway to pull it down. But then the rainy season came and the floss began absorbing water, becoming both heavier and smaller when Murph gave it one final tug and it rolled down the steps and atop Murph—crushing the life out of him.

At the viewing, Murph's casket was set low so well wishers could see him, or at least see parts that weren't welded to his beloved floss ball. His face remained just as it had at the end—with a surprised mouth-open look, eyebrows raised up high, arms wrapped around the floss and one leg stuck out at a ninety-degree angle. And that was how Murph went to his final resting place, in a box stamped Steinway, while his parents collected five dollars a head to view and ten for a picture standing next to him.

Cinders

I love to take pictures at fires. The firemen, trucks, hoses, ladders, onlookers with their concerned looks and the fires themselves, especially when the flames are roaring and the black smoke is drifting through the air with lit cinders like fireflies. I love the crackling of the fire, the smell of burnt wood but most of all I love those flying cinders.

I have a Fire website—www.myfavoritefires.com. I name the fires by date, time and location. I used to have other hobbies but since I got the fire department scanner this takes up a good deal of my time. After all, I have a regular job at our local weekly, selling ads, doing interviews, and writing a weekly feature.

I don't talk to people about my hobby except to tell them I'm a photographer and that, in my small town, is acceptable, so no one thinks anything about my taking pictures at fires because I also shoot parades, farmers markets, and local fairs.

I tried to explain this to the police when they brought me in for questioning regarding a suspicious fire. They laid out photo after photo of me at just about every fire in town. It turns out that I'm not the only fire photographer—the department has their own. They even had an old black and white one of me when I was thirteen watching my own house burn. I was holding my camera then, too.

Tassels & Brown Legs

Brown legs brown boots white tassels no socks, turquoise robe hood, trimmed in black, turquoise shorts, black trim shuffle shuffle skip skip punch punch drops of face sweat fall to canvas skips bounces in place shadow boxing crosses self

red satin hood climbs steps manager steps on bottom rope pulls up middle rope brown legs step through black boots red socks red tassels red laces skips around in circle grabs corner middle ropes kneels bows head prays crosses points up gets up

out of robes center ring staring inches apart touches them up goes to corner bell rings gloves touch and pop pop pop skip skip hook body shot body shot straight right down sees mother and wife hands to mouth gets up six count

pop pop pop skip skip dodge weave jab jab hook hook clinch hook hook cross cross skip skip back back back corner pop pop body body clinch clinch head butt separation warning jab jab jab weave jab weave weave pop pop pop pop shuffle side shuffle side swing forward pop pop pop eyebrow leaking blood shakes head

looked right roundhouse left uppercut back on ropes hands up punish body punish body hook body hook hook hook head shot head shot no return

referee waves arms hugs loser no no no winner stands ropes gloves aloft si si si crowd chant chant chant referee raises winners right arm chant chant chant blood on

turquoise robe eye closed blood dripping winner loser hug
loser raises winner's arm   mother wife hug cry

Spring Break

We were five couples, all long out of college, in St. Thomas on Spring Break while our kids were Spring Breaking it in Cancun.

Hung-over, we went to the beach and after a couple we carried our third into the water.

Mirsky, barefoot, steps on a sea urchin, screams and drops his margarita. The rest were wearing water shoes so we help him back on the beach. Someone says the only cure for the sting is urine and we talk about which one of us guys is going to pee on Mirsky's foot.

The wives want in on the action so we say what the hey and we're feeding Mirsky more margaritas.

No one thinks to call the resort doctor but we do decide to have a backgammon tournament and the winner gets to pee on Mirsky.

We've attracted a bit of attention with our raucous behavior. Rubberneckers abound. Finally, someone suggests we check on Mirsky. We look over from our tournament and he's lying where we left him but there's a man with three kids peeing on him. We leave our games and walk over. The youngest kid, about six is peeing on Mirsky's knee while the father and his two teenage sons are whizzing on the foot in just the right spot.

They finish, some of us get on their case for butting in, and Mirsky thanks them and says his pain is gone and then he tells them what great friends they are. Mirsky's attitude shows that he's gone over to the other side so we huddle and walk away, leaving him at the water's edge as the tide rolls in.

A Museum Education

I overheard a woman whisper to a man, "I like your penis." I took out my moleskin and wrote it down. We were in a large elevator in the Metropolitan Museum of Art in New York. The couple was backed up in the corner and I was pushed back also, turned sideways almost facing them but, due to my height, I only came up to the woman's shoulder and neither she or the man knew or cared I was standing there.

I followed them around and took pictures of the artwork and of them. Both wore wedding rings.

I followed them into the elevator going up and we all resumed our positions and she said, "I want your penis." I already had my notebook out and wrote that down.

We got out at the modern art floor where there was a Duane Hansen sculpture of a security guard standing three feet from the elevator door looking in. He looked real and many people asked him for directions and then felt silly when they realized.

The couple I was following walked up to another couple standing close and speaking. "Here you are," the new man said. "I thought I'd have to send the security guard after you." He pointed at the Duane Hansen and all four laughed. They all kissed hello and they changed partners and walked around.

I took pictures of all and got a lot of meaningful looks between the non-marrieds.

We rode the elevator down to the first floor and the couples changed partners again. The original couple said they had to get back to work and the other couple said they were going to grab a bite.

Back into the elevator and to the corner and the man said, "Lucky break—they both have to go to the new exhibit tonight."

"I'll get a room at the Sheraton and text you the number," she said.

I wrote this down as they exited in front of me and, as I was leaving, the elderly volunteer elevator operator touched my arm and said, "I'm only here for the conversations too." He took a small spiral from his breast pocket and showed it to me and then pointed at the hearing aid in his left ear. When the door closed I took out my moleskin and wrote that down also.

All the Presidents' Wives

The screen door was ajar and the front door opened all the way. Peeking in I saw a rough hewn square coffee table set on cedar stumps, the bark still mostly on. There was a large glass plate overflowing with smoked cigarettes, some filters, some plain with roaches mixed in.

I knew there was no one home but I yelled "Hello" anyway and then walked in and scoped out the room. The couch used to be velour but was now mostly shiny and worn cloth, the cushions uneven and sunken. The only light entered from the two windows and the front door.

On one wall was a large print of "The Scream" and next to it a print of kittens and yarn—the yarn balls all different colors. I figured the kittens went up first and the response following. Off to the left was a stairway going up with a half dozen balusters missing, lying askew on the floor.

There was a large yellow bean bag chair that had seen better days and, like the couch, it faced what was left of a giant flat screen TV. Glass littered the worn oak floor.

I walked through the living room and saw police tape had cordoned off the dining room with the dining table and chairs flipped over in the rear of the room.

There were the chalk outlines where the two bodies had been and the stain of red blood now turned brown. The first body was large, perhaps a German Shepard, and the other, smaller but compact and I figured Cockapoo.

The dining room walls had mounted plates with portraits of all the First Ladies but they were untouched.

I didn't need to go into any other rooms. I saw what I came for and left, but not before grabbing a baluster and flinging it into the dining room, cracking Abigail Adams.

Chilling Memories

On my weekly train rides from New Haven to New York I always look at the projects in Bridgeport that I grew up in. There are fifteen to twenty two story flat-roofed buildings— each building housing eight families. Last month I saw a half dozen of the apartments with windows and doors boarded over and each subsequent week there were more and more until yesterday when Marina Village was a ghost town of asphalt and brick, with large bulldozers, a wrecking ball on a crane and a line of dump trucks lined up, sentinel like, to take my childhood away.

I picked up my car at the New Haven railroad station and drove back to Bridgeport and parked in a tight space in the parking lot, something I wouldn't have done before. I walked through the asphalt jungle, as John Huston so aptly named his movie.

It was dusk, the cloud cover thick and low as I passed a couple of buildings heading towards my old one. I saw a blur of orange and walked closer and there was a group of twenty or so men in orange jump suits with the word "Prisoner" stenciled across their backs. They were a mixture of black, Puerto Rican, and white. Some were exercising, some playing cards, a few talking in small groups and most were smoking. I grew up with them all and I walked closer and they turned and stood as a barrier to keep me from entering.

"Hey Joey, Leroy, Juan, Mickey," I called. No one answered and I walked closer and their faces were young faces on old bodies and when the light struck a different way, their faces became old—older and harder looking than our age should have fostered. They resumed their game playing ritual without responding to me and I walked around the building, planning on going to mine the back way. I heard the train go by and the din of the cars on the adjacent interstate and I wondered how I lived with all the noise.

I stopped to watch a group of teens in the corner of the parking lot shooting craps against the curb. I knew them all and one was me, looking back at me, as he blew on the dice and rolled them, then picked up the bills in the center and rolled again.

I moved on and had no problem finding my apartment, my mother sitting on the stoop with the next door neighbor, drinking coffee, their wash in baskets ready to hang on the line. The bricks in the building moved in ripples. My bedroom window was not boarded nor was the door. In order to get in and look around my mother or our neighbor would have to move aside, but neither did. I saw my brother looking out the bedroom window at me and I waved but he didn't respond.

I headed back to my car and there were now all the people from the Village out and about and I felt as if I were walking a gauntlet getting back to my car, which had a couple of hoods from my youth sitting on the hood. "Move," I said and they did, but towards me, and their faces were no more the young faces but drinkers' faces with veined red noses, rheumy eyes and their walk was more of a jailhouse shuffle.

I drove home to my comfortable life in the New Haven burbs. In the morning, I went out to the garage to get my car and saw that it had graffiti all over it but we didn't call it graffiti back then. *Jew boy, faggot, loser, creep, punk* and other reminders written in crayon and chalk that I hadn't noticed last night when I walked to my car.

The following week, I saw from the train the wrecking crew had done their job and only the dozers remained and it seemed like such a small piece of property to hold so many people and memories.

Bad Man

I am running away from the Bad Man. He's threatened my knees and eyes and it's all over a misunderstanding. His dog followed me, I didn't dognap him. I'm out of shape and I stop and look around for a place to hide and spot an alley. I sit on a garbage can laying on its side trying to catch my breath but the smell of garbage is overpowering.

Suddenly a cab slows down for a yellow traffic light and I run out to the street and lift my hand. The driver nods me over and I heft myself up after I open the door.

I freeze. Bad Man is sitting on the far side and reaches over, grabs my shirt and pulls me into the cab with him.

"Why are you chasing me?" I ask, pretending I don't know.

He pulls me closer—we're staring at each other and he coughs in my face and his putrid garlic, cigar and anchovy breath almost knock me out. He coughs again and starts laughing and lets me go and I fall out of the cab just as it starts to move through the green light. I roll over and over and am stopped by the curb.

I get up from the road and run across the street. I sneak a peek and see the cab continue on. I hobble over to the dog bowl in front of a dress shop, kneel down and wash my face and neck with the dog water and feel good about replacing Bad Man's smell with dog odor.

Years later, enough time has passed, so I don't think about Bad Man anymore and I'm in my "I Chocolate Cover Everything!" kiosk dipping Peep bunnies into the milk chocolate when I hear, "You got enough dark chocolate to dip these?" I look up and it's him—large unlit stogie in the corner of his mouth and he's holding out a wooden fruit crate filled with anchovies and garlic cloves.

I knock over the drying Peeps getting out the door and start running. I hear heavy footsteps behind me and trip over a Schnauzer and land on my head.

The last thing I remember is Bad Man kneeling by me. I smell his once familiar deadly odor wafting over me as he asks if I can have his order ready by the weekend.

Color Coordination Rules

Melborne walked five steps and quickly tapped his left heel with his right toe and continued on. He was in his mid-fifties, dressed nattily and stopped at the same flower stand every morning for his boutonnière—a blue daisy.

One day he added a double tap to the right side of his nose with his index finger whenever he crossed a street. At times he had to shift a bag from right hand to left.

Weeks later he began speaking with a low "mmm" before beginning whatever it was he had to say and that was followed by tapping his pencil eraser against his front teeth while on the phone listening.

Melborne held steady with these habits for quite a while and then one day he stopped at a different flower stand and bought a yellow rose.

He no longer tapped or "mmm'd" but had taken to knuckle cracking, whistling, ear probing and an occasional hop upon hearing a thunderclap.

Discussion of My Night Patrol with the Guys from the Station While Having Drinks

I may have stopped the Corvette that night so I could check out the smiling blonde in the passenger's seat with her hair whipping in the wind.

I may have cracked his tail light with my baton as I approached the driver's side window.

"Do you know who I am?" he protested and I may have told him he was the guy driving with a broken taillight and was going to get a ticket and he best shut his pie hole and step out of the car. I may have quick frisked him and then I had the blonde step out and put her hands on the hood of the car.

I could tell she was used to having a man's hands run over her body. She stood still and never complained, even when I felt her crotch and reached inside her thong and pulled out a baggie of white powder.

He threatened he'd have my badge while she promised me the world. I liked her option better so I may have cuffed him and thrown him in the back seat of my patrol car and had her follow me home in the Vette.

Five Minutes Can Make a Difference

This morning I woke at 5:25, five minutes earlier than my usual 5:30, looked over and saw Elaine in her usual covered head to toe under her sheet and I went to the bathroom to take my shower. We have an old-fashioned bathroom, claw-foot tub, and shower with a circular metal post to wrap the curtain around and a one-time fashionable powder blue toilet and sink.

That's not the bathroom I was standing in. This was chrome and glass with a jetted tub for two and a glass shower with a seat and multiple shower heads. The toilet and sinks were crimson to match the shower and tub as well as the paint job and ceramic tiles.

There was an electric razor and after shave lotion neither of which I use and hand crèmes and face lotions with French names. I walked back out of the bathroom and into the bedroom. The lump in the bed appeared larger than Elaine's lump and there was someone lying on my side of the bed.

I ran out to the unfamiliar hall, opened the front door and peered around to see the house number which was 22. Just as the house alarm went off, Mr. Lump came running out of the bedroom with a golf club (I believe it was a 3 iron) and he demanded to know what I was doing in his house.

He looked at my nakedness and held the club like he was going to swing a baseball bat. "Wrong grip for a 3," I said.

"Angie, call the police and tell them we have a naked burglar in the house."

Her curiosity got the better of her and out of the bedroom she walked with her cell phone, wearing a terry cloth robe. "Hold on a minute, honey, this guy can't hurt a flea with his club," pointing to my privates.

Mr. Lump put his arm around Mrs. Lump and they walked back into the bedroom, giggling.

"Oh by the way," he said pointing. "There's a jump suit in the garage I use to change my oil. You can wear it to go back to wherever you're supposed to be."

I heard the bed creak and looked around. I took a glass paperweight from their collection on the desk and walked out to the garage, looking for the jumpsuit.

Irma Likes Her Blessings Elaine Likes Her Humpty

Elaine:

My friend Irma says everything's a blessing: "I'm sorry about your cat but it's probably a blessing in disguise." "Your wallet—well with that horrid picture of you on your license you should count it as a blessing." "You burned the cake while talking to me on the phone? You don't need the calories—it's a blessing."

And on and on. She ought to count her blessings that all of us girlfriends don't make fun of her every time she uses the word, but we have talked about approaching her with the concept.

I have to tread a little lighter than the others since I've been fucking her husband for a couple of years now. Notice, I don't say 'having an affair' or use the term 'lovemaking' or any other term of endearment about what we're doing. Deep down he and I come from the same gutter rat background and these suburban cookouts, cocktail parties and get-togethers are more than either of us can bear, so we fuck.

Irma ought to count her blessings that I'm the one taking the bite out of his stinger leaving her to plan her seasonal wardrobe and events, her two book clubs, the garden club, and her choir practice.

Mirsky:

I still get it on with Elaine but she's a creature of habit and waits for the evening news to be over on Wednesday (Hump Day) and then excuses herself and showers and puts on something from Victoria's Secret and calls to me. Every once in a while we come home a little loaded on a weekend and get it on but Elaine always admonishes me that we're not adding that day to our regular routine. "Consider this a bonus night," she says, "I want to look forward to Humpty (as she's taken to calling it) all week so I can give you my everything and I'm sure you feel the same way."

Elaine:

I went to lunch and then shopping with Irma today and my taking the time to be with her was a blessing as was my willingness to share a Cobb Salad with anchovies and the third blessing came when I talked her out of buying crotchless panties online and going for the bondage toys instead.

Crotchless panties are my thing with her husband and I don't plan on sharing that. Blessings be damned.

Pray and Confess or Else

"Time Heals" my father said as we were approaching my high school in his beat up old red pickup. He slowed but didn't stop in front of the school, leaned across me and opened my door and shoved me out onto the hard-packed dirt and stone road with the contents of my backpack scattering to the whims of the wind. I struggled to my knees and watched his trail of dust and venom heading towards parts unknown.

Mom still uses the same dinner plates—three sections, two for vegetables and the largest for the main course.

"Pray," he'd command as my two sisters, mother and I sat after all our plates were filled.

"Thank you dear Father/husband for all of your hard work and sacrifices in order to put food on our plates and a roof over our heads. We love, revere and bless you even though we don't deserve you."

Then one by one, before we ate, we did our confessions.

"Daughter Number One, confess," and so on down the line, including Mom. If the confession was sufficient then the person could start eating. If Dad deemed it lame he'd grab the food from one of the sections, fling it to the floor and give the offender another chance. There were times when one of us kids or even Mom had all of our food scooped away and went to bed hungry.

Jimmy Beam, our Shepherd mix, sat shaking awaiting my father's okay to eat the food. Even though the dog's dish was only an arm's length away Dad still threw the food on the floor causing more work for Mom.

At breakfast this morning, Mom, bruised from the night's argument, made pancakes. Pancakes are our Sunday dinner meal as decreed by my Dad. He sat fuming at her rule-breaking and drummed his dirty and broken fingernails on the table—the creases on his hands filled with unwashed axle grease. His drumming became louder as a warning to my mother whose bruised face was painful to look at.

She filled our plates, then hers and then put down the fork and grabbed two pancakes with her hand and slapped them onto my father's plate while staring back at him. She blocked his arm as he reached for a pancake.

"Pray," she said, "Thank you my dear wife for this wonderful food you made this morning even though your body is sore from yet another one of my drunken nights. Thank you for putting up with me and my stupid rules and before I eat I'd like to confess in front of you and our children."

Dad sat stone silent with an "I'm going to kill this woman look".

Mom said, "Pray."

But he said nothing. Mom reached over, grabbed his pancakes and flung them to the floor next to his chair. "Go," she said to Jimmy Beam and motioned with her hand and as his breakfast was being lapped up Dad stood, knocking over his chair and started towards Mom.

"Get in the truck," he snarled at me.

"Finish your breakfast first," Mom said taking the ice pick from her apron pocket and holding it at the ready.

Leaving my pancakes, I stood to get my backpack. With fists balled and face twisted Dad again stepped towards Mom. I grabbed the ice pick from her hand and jabbed it into the kitchen table between me and Dad. He turned and walked

out to the truck and I touched Mom's cheek and followed
him and got in.

Birthday Beer

My wife called and told me to come home. I finished my birthday beer and drove home and the driveway and yard were filled with cars. Some surprise birthday party. I grabbed a drink from someone's hand and walked around the gathering. I looked and these were not my closest friends, in fact, not my current friends at all but people I'd played tricks on, rolled over in business deals, and spoken against to others. They climbed the deck stairs and I was people-pushed into my living room and told to stand in a square taped onto the floor. A dozen people spoke of my less than honorable associations with them, someone blew an air horn and a trap door opened. I tumbled down into the dark expecting to hit either the concrete basement floor or a body of water but neither happened and I continued to fall and this is day four of my birthday free fall.

My brother appears next to me, falling alongside, and makes fun of me and says that he can dream in color and I can't. You're right I tell him but I can dream in 3D and he tells me I'm lying and I say prove it.

A fisher cat's been pacing back and forth across my front lawn going from one neighbor to another and I have to believe, since I have no pets, my house is of no interest to him except when my daughter drops her eight month old baby off on her way to work. The fisher cat stops and watches. He resumes his pacing but is back at 5pm sharp when my daughter picks the baby up.

I've had enough of the way things are going so I decide to run for Congress. My speeches are stirring, money is flowing in and my Republican opponent is dead in the water and thinking of dropping out. I'm star quality—a shoe-in and everything's fine until the report comes in of me and the villagers in Iraq. I dye my hair and move to Denver.

Every night I open the door to my garage and check that the garage doors are down. Each night when I do this I expect to see a grizzly bear on his hind legs baring his teeth at me. My wife says I'm foolish. Tonight when I went to check, the garage doors were open, and I heard a god-awful screeching and it was the fisher cat ripping my scarecrow apart.

I'm back at my house and the birthday party is in full swing. I ask for a birthday beer and my wife says for me to go stand on the marked square and she'll bring it over.

Acknowledgments

Grateful acknowledgment is made to the following publications in which these stories appeared either with the same title and form, or different:

Ascent Aspirations Anthology: 'A Visit From Grammy'
The Airgonaut: 'Code Red', 'Dummy' and 'With a Wink and a Nod'
Bartleby Snopes: 'Columbia Market'
Beautiful Losers: 'Changing of the Guard'
Bending Genres: 'Too Many Uncles'
Blue Fifth Notebook: 'Trade'
(b)OINK: 'Birthday Beer'
Boston Literary Magazine: 'The Blame Game' and 'Color Co-ordination Rules'
Brilliant Flash and *Fiction Zero Flash*: 'This Has Got to Stop'
Brilliant Flash Fiction: 'Goodbye Already'
Cosmonauts Avenue: 'Cool Water'
Degenerate Literature: 'All the President's Wives' and 'I Am Not the Marathon Man'
Doorknobs and Body Paint: 'Spice of Life'
The Drabble: 'Creeps', 'Speaking of My Father'* and 'Superpowers'
Earl of Plaid: 'Lemon Pledge'
Fiction Attic Press: 'TSA: Here to Serve'
Fiction on the Web: 'Wallflower Solution'

Fictive Dream: 'Columbia Market Delivers'
50 Word Stories: 'Uncle Harry's Last Magic Trick'
Firefly Magazine: 'Mother of the Bride' (originally published
   as 'A Part of the Landscape')
five2one magazine: 'A Museum Education'
Flash Fiction Magazine: 'I Had No Choice. I Had to
   Let My Cleaning Lady Go'
Flash Fiction Magazine: 'Cars, Trains and Smoke Rings'
Flash International: 'Finding Grandma Pearl'
Foliate Oak: 'Mom on the USO Circuit'
Gravel: 'Bad Man' and 'Tassels and Brown Legs'
The Ham: 'Epilogue'
The Ham and *Entropy*: 'A Great Multi-Tasker'
Heavy Feather Review: 'Dear Editor'
Jellyfish Review: 'Dental Floss Debate: Good vs. Not So Good'
   and 'Five Minutes Can Make a Difference'
JMWW: 'Another Day at the Office'
Literary Orphans: 'Beat the Mirror' and 'Floaters'
Lost Balloon: 'Winter Walks'
Matter Press: 'Pray and Confess or Else'
No Extra Words Podcast: 'Dean's Dilemma'
Not Your Mother's Breast Milk: 'Chilling Memories'
101 word stories: 'Destination Wedding'
Pure Slush: 'Jimbo'
Pure Slush ('5' anthology): 'Spring'
r.k.v.r.y.: 'Fantasy Party' (originally published as 'Higher
   and Harder')
Spelk: 'Cinders', 'Deal or no Deal', 'I Have a Problem',
   'Irma Likes Her Blessings Elaine Likes Her Humpty'
   and 'Semantics'
Star 82 Review: 'Stalemate'
Sweater Weather: 'Drivers' Rules'
Thrice Fiction: 'The Woman with the Juicy Fruit Breath'
Tribe: 'Chica Radar'

Tuck: 'I Didn't Have a Ready Answer'
Unbroken Journal: 'The Only Hope of the Jews' **
The Wagon Magazine: 'Father Panik Village'
We Are a Website: 'A Pinball Day in the Projects'
Yellow Mama: 'Kiss Kiss'

* Editor's Pick
** Pushcart-nominated

Thanks

I would like to thank my wife Sandra for the hours she spent editing and reading my stories. She is abundant with her praise and fearless with her criticism.

I would like to give a big thanks to all of my writer friends who are so good I learn something every time I read one of their stories or they comment on mine.

I would like to acknowledge Mirsky and Elaine for being available for yet another book.

Lastly, but not last, my publisher, Matt Potter, whose creativity, good humor and extreme patience makes him a pleasure to know and work with.

About the Author

Paul Beckman is a retired air traffic controller and real estate entrepreneur. His published books include two collections: *Peek* (Big Table Publishing) and *Come! Meet My Family and other stories* (Weighted Anchor Press); a novella, *Lovers and Other Mean People* (Sugar Mule Press); and a chapbook, *Maybe I Ought to Sit in a Dark Room for a While* (Ink, Sweat and Tears). He has had over 350 of his stories published in print, online, and via audio, in *Literary Orphans, Connecticut Review, Playboy, Matter Press, Litro, Thrice Fiction, The Airgonaut, Jellyfish Review*, and *r.kv.r.y*, as well as many others. He runs the monthly FBomb flash fiction reading series at KGB in New York City. His story 'Brother Speak' was selected for the 2018 Norton Microfiction Anthology. Additionally, Paul was one of the winners of the Best Small Fictions 2016, and the editor's choice for 2016 Fiction Southeast.

Also from TRUTH SERUM PRESS and PURE SLUSH BOOKS

http://truthserumpress.net/catalogue/

- *Inklings* by Irene Buckler
  978-1-925536-41-6 (paperback) 978-1-925536-42-3 (eBook)
- *Track Tales* by Mercedes Webb-Pullman
  978-1-925536-35-5 (paperback) 978-1-925536-36-2 (eBook)
- *On the Bitch* by Matt Potter
  978-1-925536-45-4 (paperback) 978-1-925536-46-1 (eBook)

  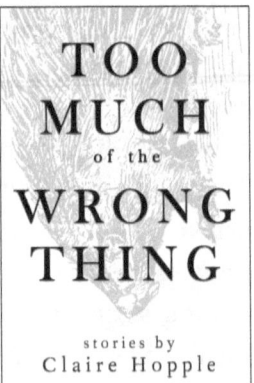

- *Happy² Pure Slush Vol. 15*
  978-1-925536-39-3 (paperback) 978-1-925536-40-9 (eBook)
- *Lust: 7 Deadly Sins Vol. 1*
  978-1-925536-47-8 (paperback) 978-1-925536-48-5 (eBook)
- *Too Much of the Wrong Thing* by Claire Hopple
  978-1-925536-33-1 (paperback) 978-1-925536-34-8 (eBook)

Also from TRUTH SERUM PRESS and EVERYTIME PRESS

http://truthserumpress.net/catalogue/

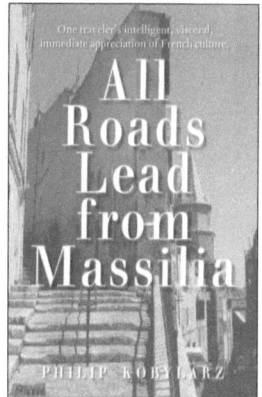 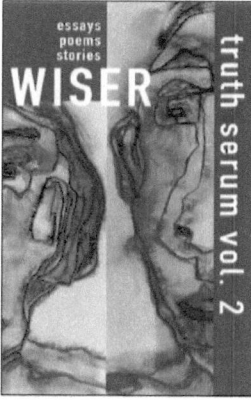 

- *All Roads Lead from Massilia* by Philip Kobylarz
  978-1-925536-27-0 (paperback) 978-1-925536-28-7 (eBook)
- *Wiser Truth Serum Vol. #2*
  978-1-925536-31-7 (paperback) 978-1-925536-32-4 (eBook)
- *True Truth Serum Vol. #1*
  978-1-925536-29-4 (paperback) 978-1-925536-30-0 (eBook)

- *Hello Berlin!* by Jason S. Andrews
  978-1-925536-11-9 (paperback) 978-1-925536-12-6 (eBook)
- *Deer Michigan* by Jack C. Buck
  978-1-925536-25-6 (paperback) 978-1-925536-26-3 (eBook)
- *Rain Check* by Levi Andrew Noe
  978-1-925536-09-6 (paperback) 978-1-925536-10-2 (eBook)

Also from TRUTH SERUM PRESS

http://truthserumpress.net/catalogue/

- *Luck and Other Truths* by Richard Mark Glover
  978-1-925101-77-5 (paperback) 978-1-925536-04-1 (eBook)
- *happyme@t.us* by Kim Conklin
  978-1-925536-07-2 (paperback) 978-1-925536-08-9 (eBook)
- *What Came Before* by Gay Degani
  978-1-925536-05-8 (paperback) 978-1-925536-06-5 (eBook)

- *Based on True Stories* by Matt Potter
  978-1-925101-75-1 (paperback) 978-1-925101-76-8 (eBook)
- *The Miracle of Small Things* by Guilie Castillo Oriard
  978-1-925101-73-7 (paperback) 978-1-925101-74-4 (eBook)
- *La Ronde* by Townsend Walker
  978-1-925101-64-5 (paperback) 978-1-925101-65-2 (eBook)